Regina

Wild Innocence

A Tale from the Eighties

Thank you

by

Moody Holiday

Moody Holiday

Wasteland Press
Louisville, KY USA
www.wastelandpress.com

Wild Innocence: A Tale from the Eighties
By Moody Holiday

First Printing-March, 2003
Book design by Wasteland Press

ISBN: 0-9729186-4-7

MHoliday™

The MHoliday design is a trademark of the author.

Printed In The U.S.A.

TWO FATHERS

By

Moody Holiday

One father known only till three,
Taking credit for biology.
Passing down a gift to write,
Symbolically blind, now having sight.
New father came in at the age of three,
Reconstructed my biology.
Organized my thoughts for this "thing" called life.
Strong and articulate through systems and strife.
Rejected the notions of "It's a man's world."
Standing tall and statuesque, no longer a girl.
Dear father I thank you for endless integrity,
Scripting pen to paper I finally see,
I write from two sets of biology,
One bearing life and one setting me free.
I LOVE YOU DADDY

Table of Contents

The Encounter	7
Quiet Respite	31
Portia	35
Wayne Valley High	39
Night Vision	46
The Test	50
Vision of Him	65
Devil's Dormancy	75
Something Old Something New	82
Beyond Control	85
St. Amelia's	99
Time Flies	105
Alex	113
I Dream Alex	126
Exit Wounds	130
Hope	132
Butterfly	152

Acknowledgments

The Encounter

St. James Prep, 1980. A cold crisp smell in the air was a sign to many New Jersey natives that it was going to snow. I didn't care how much snow fell that night because nothing could keep me from seeing Derrick play basketball. Besides, I lived a stone's throw away from St. James and I was going to lie to my parents no matter how late I stayed out.

My mounting love and affection for Derrick didn't need Cupid's arrow. He's the type of brother any woman would drop her panties for upon sight. His ancestral legacy commanded hair as fine as silk from the Blackfoot Indian Tribe. If Derrick stood up in church and proclaimed that he had Indian in his family, I would have stood up and shouted, "Amen!"

His cocoa brown skin glistened with life unfettered by stress or acne. He stood long and lean at six feet tall and weighed two hundred and fifteen pounds. His upper thighs were chiseled to perfection and his muscular calves ruggedly supported his six pack stomach and sculpted chest. When he smiled, I instantly held my breath to contain his masculine energy. The release leaves me fulfilled like the air at the dawn of a new day. My heart is pumping right now just thinking about him, but that's how he makes me feel when I'm around him, girly, giddy and sexy.

The game plan for the evening was to play it cool and sophisticated. My hormones were raging and I was ripe for some flirtatious titillation. One last check in the circular compact mirror heightened my need for Derrick. The "do" was done, slicked back in a pony tail, not a follicle out of place. I used a small eyebrow brush to sculpt my baby hair into four little swirls like Betty Boop. Maybeline Dial A Lash mascara whipped my lashes out long and thick like a brand new baby doll. Gloria Vanderbilt Jeans and a burgundy v-neck sweater with matching boots from the Village adorned my frame. No turning back, I walked up the stairs taking in the blaring noise from the gym.

Tonight was a critical game and the standing room only capacity crowd gave it more credibility. Fans, young and old were chanting and clapping for St. James Prep. Blue and white pom poms shook to the frantic beat of the drums. Fog horns blared from every quadrant. Painted faces adorned the wild boys of St. James. They were loyal students who never missed a game or the chance to entertain. The young men of St. James Prep rallied behind their team chanting, "Defense, defense!" Despite the excitement of the electrified crowd, I stayed focused. I walked straight into the gym and down the sidelines. My need for the moment was to concentrate on my Love Jones. I passed the wanna-bees, the nerds and the curious boys staring me down as I walked past their wandering eyes. I reached the middle section of the court and climbed each bleacher with cool confidence. I kept to myself and shied away from the cat and scratch girls. Those bitches threw down in a minute if they thought you were after their imaginary boyfriends. Half of them looked like a good recipe for a witch's brew; spiked hair, pointy black shoes and ten pounds of make up. Without my girls to back me up, I had to stay away from any potential catfights.

Like any other true spectator, I needed to be at the top of the rafters to see the entire spectacle. The guys from the neighborhood were up there selling wolf tickets and gossiping about the girls in the crowd. I chose to stand by the young bookies. With three to one odds, they were just as focused as I was to win one for the Gipper. With all the excitement in the air, there was also bound to be a good fight or two to compliment the game.

Huge pennants adorned the entire perimeter of the gymnasium ceiling. Parochial Division Championships were lined up next to each other from 1968 through 1971 and from 1973 to 1979. For St. James, it was an accomplished achievement considering other rival schools like St. Anthony's Prep, Essex Catholic and Immaculate High School. Below, veteran North Orange police officers stood guard in front of the entry doors and on the opposite side. Although the right side of the gymnasium did not offer an exit, the police had to be ready in the event of a physical fight.

Young and old were at this game. Babies, not old enough to stand the magnified noise, were bounced up and down on their fathers' laps. They were dressed in tiny blue and white sweatshirts. Miniature pennants were shoved in their little hands. The fact that they were infants did little to deter their attendance. It was their destiny to be introduced to St. James Prep and ultimately become students.

Old men with black felt hats and wool coats stood like frantic stock exchange runners shouting, "Box out, you son of bitch!" Another yelled, "Hey! You call that a foul you stinking ref, don't make me come down there and shove my foot up your ass!" These old dudes went to every game ready to hurl insults like they had Torrets' Syndrome.

My favorite fan and nursing home reject was Bottle Cap Willie. He could barely see through his thick glasses, but he knew when to get up and when to sit his ass down. With his cane in tow as a cheering accessory, every now and then somebody would get a quick jab to the back of the head with Willie's splintered brown cane. If you dared to turn around, Willie cursed you out like it was your fault. His reputation gained him a four by four invisible clearance section like box seats at a major league baseball game.

Bottle Cap Willie had one faithful friend and head honcho named Danny Dentures. He had bad breath, a dusty black coat and a wicked set of dentures that needed serious refurbishing. When the game got too intense for old man Danny, he juggled those dentures in his mouth to calm himself down. Willie and Danny were a sight to see. Danny must have dropped his dentures under the bleachers a million times and it took blind ass Willie half of the game to find them.

During a heated game against Essex Catholic two weeks ago, Willie used his cane as a hockey stick to slide them out from under the second row. The dirty dentures slid across the court during an inbound pass to St. James. The referee had to call a time out to let Danny get the hair and gum infested dentures off the floor. An extra five minutes was allowed for a quick mop up. Nobody seemed to mind. Willie and Danny were part of the school spirit and a lesson in respect for the elderly. Besides, they were also a great comedy act to watch. Even though they were a pain in the ass, they didn't mean any harm and that's what made them so loveable.

I took final position and began to search for him, but he was no where to be found. My heart started beating rapidly until I noticed two players from St. James running out of the locker room. The second player was Derrick. Just the sight of him caused me to quietly exhale. I wondered what happened to him and if he was alright. Even if he was slightly hurt, I was going to see to it that he felt one hundred percent better with my warm embrace.

Suddenly, a loud noise distracted everyone's attention away from the game. A small fight erupted on the opposite side of the gym. Dominick, a loyal North Orange cop for more than fourteen years, jetted up the bleachers, removed the instigator by the collar, spun him through the double doors and into the lobby. Back-up officers were waiting for the instigator. They grabbed him under his armpits and carried him out the doors into the raging snowstorm. As the officers wiped the snow off their leather jackets, they laughed and gave each other the infamous nod, especially Dominick. He seemed annoyed that his hair got wet because it always looked picture perfect. We all knew the ejected jerk got smacked around and sent home to his momma slipping and sliding through the snow. Cops did that in my day, so it was standard to mind your own business. At a minimum, it kept teen pranks down and elevated other types of corruption.

Despite the spectacle, I began to focus on the object of my desire. I took another deep breath and stared at him. Derrick filled my lungs and took up every ounce of my being. On a daily basis, I imagined him in multiple fantasies. Thoughts of him consumed my academic and social existence. I fashioned a world of daydreams in his awesome splendor. While learning Greek mythology, Derrick reminded me of Zeus, in the color of cocoa brown. There were days that I was so confused by him that I could not concentrate on simple tasks. One day I put my Noxzema in the hamper and my washcloth in the cabinet. I laughed at myself, because my carelessness was a compliment of my love and devotion to him. The anticipation for his touch and not knowing how we would ever become an item drove me into flights of fantasy. They were fueled by four chance encounters that sealed our fate.

The first encounter was at the South Orange Library. I was perplexed over algebraic equations until Derrick came to my rescue. He walked up to the table and looked at me. A simple hello was his calling card. He sat down and offered to help. I stared at him feverishly as the words he spoke began to form life within me.

I felt warm on the inside and I could hear the pulse in my wrist beat on the library table. I had no idea what he was talking about regarding algebra, but it sounded beautiful. I stared at him intensely and registered every inch of his face in my brain. He had soft hair that swept and curled in different directions. Some of his hair spiked straight up like he couldn't tame it, perhaps a little pomade would do the trick, but he looked too rugged for beeswax. His eyebrows were smooth and thick and they complimented his almond-shaped eyes. The first time he smiled was magical.

He looked warm and sincere like he appreciated my company. His energy gave me new life. Because of him, I began to smile more, but only when there were thoughts of him in my head. After giving it careful consideration, I damn near smiled all the time, but never at home. As Derrick spoke, I watched his lips ease and relax. The more time he spent with me, the more comfortable we became together. Our eyes locked more than five times and it suspended us into a trance. We were caught in a visual embrace that I did not want to let go of for a million years. I wondered what his eyes were saying to me and if they were inviting me to say something that made sense. I could not speak because I was so asphyxiated by his presence. His skin was so silky that I wanted to stroke his face and ask him if he used Noxzema or Ivory Soap. I remembered thinking, "Damn, he is so fine," but he wasn't a pretty boy.

He was rough around the edges and his eyes had a mysterious element to them, like he was hiding something from me. I knew then that I would do just about anything to unlock the mystery in him. As he spoke to me, I went along with his problem solving until he was finished. Sure, my homework was done, but I didn't comprehend a damn thing, except his kindness and physiology. Derrick slid my notebook and pencil back to me and I put them in my book bag. I took a deep breath and folded my hands. I smiled and then laughed softly wondering what I should say to him so he wouldn't leave. He told me he wasn't in a rush, so we went to the periodical lounge section and talked. It was a simple conversation about common acquaintances and teachers. I could not keep my eyes off him and Derrick could not keep his eyes off me. He got up one time to help an elderly woman pick up some change she dropped on the floor. She thanked him, gave me a wink and said, "The two of you make a lovely couple."

He went along with her compliment and sat closer to me. He put his arm around me and replied to her, "We look even better now."

She chuckled in delight and said, "Now be good and stay out of trouble."

Derrick whispered this time so not to disturb the patrons and said, "Yes ma'am!" He also mimicked a military salute to the old woman to enhance his witty personality. He was smooth in his approach and I was on fire from the feel of his touch. It was also the first time I was stimulated by a guy's fragrance. Every nerve ending in my body seemed to pulsate with each breath we took and the pure physical connection of feeling him rest on my shoulder took me into a deeper frenzy.

Time was running away from us as the light faded through the library windows. Derrick had to go to basketball practice so he offered to carry my book bag to the bus stop. He was kind enough to wait until the bus came and watched me as I boarded. As the bus pulled off, he waved goodbye as I continued to stare at him. I strained my neck to see which direction he walked and whispered his name under my breath. Surely a guy as fine as Derrick had to have a girlfriend, but I never asked and I didn't care. I wanted to see him again, but he never asked me for my number. I thought to myself, "Hmm, good thing…," because our phone was cut off.

He only knew the name of my school and that I also played basketball. He mentioned coming to one of my games, but I didn't take him seriously. I felt so stupid for not asking him for his phone number, but I didn't want to appear aggressive. It was also the first time I felt an overwhelming need to kiss a boy.

The next encounter was at the Livingston Mall. Thank God I was by myself and wearing a new outfit from Persuasions. I let Derrick notice me first, a risk that was daring for me, because I would have cried forty nights if he didn't see me. He was leaving the mall with his mother, an activity that real teens avoided on any given day, but he seemed to enjoy his mother's company. He called my name and I looked up at him pretending to be surprised.

"Hey, Derrick right?" He seemed pleased that I remembered his name.

"What's up Shanelle? Hey, meet my mom, Ms. Johnson."

She smiled at me and extended her hand. I shook her hand and did the thing my mother taught me so well.

"It's nice to meet you. Taking in some shopping with your handsome son?" She seemed to admire my courtesies.

"Yes, sweetheart, you might say that, if he can just choose something."

Derrick chimed in to avoid embarrassment. "Ok mom, don't tell my business."

I stared at the both of them intently. They looked blissfully happy, unlike the world unraveling for me that year. I thought to myself, "Are people really this happy?" Looking at the two of them reminded me of picture perfect bliss.

Derrick politely asked his mother to sit on a bench. He signaled for me to wait with his pointer finger. My heart began to beat so slow that I felt like I was frozen in time. He walked up to me and said, "I've been thinking about you ever since I saw you at the library. This time, I'm not going to let you get away without giving me your number."

I wanted to beam with lust, but my heart sank to the ground. I thought to myself, "How could I tell him I didn't have a phone number?"

Quickly thinking of an escape from the phone number, I said, "I have a game tomorrow at five thirty, can you come?"

He looked surprised and said, "Sure, I would love to come see you play."

I started to get anxious about the phone number and said, "It was nice meeting you Ms. Johnson, see you tomorrow Derrick." I headed out of the mall and caught the bus back to North Orange.

The long ride home was enough time to go over every detail of our conversation. I leaned my head against the metal bars as I closed my eyes and thought, "Did I say the right thing? Did I smile? Was I polite to his mother? Did I look nice to him?" Despite my self-critique, I desperately hoped that Derrick would come to my game. Lucky for me, he did come and he was by himself. I didn't have a great offensive game, but I didn't care. He was invited to my world and accepted the invitation. I was thrilled at the thought of it and couldn't wait for the game to be over. He waited for me in the parking lot and I immediately got excited the moment I spotted his car. I walked through the exit doors still damp from my shower. I jumped into the front seat and my perfume was the first thing he mentioned when I got in his car.

"You smell so good, what are you wearing?"

I teased him and said, "Oh, a little bit of this and that."

He stared at me so hard that silence overcame us. The sound of my goose down bomber jacket brushing up against the rest of my coat was the only noise between us. We looked at each other simultaneously and then started laughing. I felt so silly not knowing what to say and I couldn't believe he couldn't come up with a good line or two. I asked him if he was nervous and he replied, "Yeah, you make me nervous, Shanelle."

I stared at him wide eyed and asked, "Why?" His face got really serious and he told me that I was on his mind all the time. He also wanted to know what "we" should do about our situation. I put my head down not knowing how to react or what to say. My heart was racing so fast, I thought I was going to pass out on the floor of his car. The paramedics would have called in a DOA teen with an active pulsating pelvic intact and untouched. All I knew was that he smelled so good and it was the same familiar scent he was wearing in the library. He put his hand on mine and said, "Anyway, thanks for inviting me to your game, I had a great time watching you play."

I thanked him and kept my head glued to the floor. Derrick offered to take me home and I accepted. Little did I know the distraction of police sirens and their cherry bomb lights would taint my third encounter with him. Derrick didn't ask any questions as he pulled up in front of my house. There were rumors about my brother and anyone who knew somebody in North Orange heard about him. I always wondered if people thought differently of me because of my brother's reputation. Derrick politely asked if he could see me again and I decided that I would give him one honest answer.

"Look, thanks so much for taking me home, but I don't have a phone and I don't know when we'll be able to talk. I do know that I want to see you again."

With that, Derrick wrote his phone number down and placed it in the palm of my hand. He used his other hand to seal the number shut by closing my hand into a fist.

"It's up to you Shanelle," Derrick said. "Call me, or come to some of my games, I would love to see you again."

I clutched the number like it was a winning lottery ticket. Two things were sure, I was feelin' him and he was definitely feelin' me.

Rumors started swirling about us and word got back to him that his girl Portia wanted to get to know me better. Little did she know that I was a fighter and I was ready for her anytime, anyplace. I called Derrick a few times from my girlfriend's house and each conversation lasted until the early morning. We seemed to have a destiny that no one could ever understand. He wanted to be a doctor and I wanted to be a legislator. We were far beyond our years, but it was a good feeling to know that I was not alone in the world. We had common goals like going to grad school even though neither one of us was prepared to graduate high school. We loved children and strong families, even though mine was crumbling around me. We also talked about the possibility of being boyfriend and girlfriend. The more we talked, the more I wanted him in every way. He was happy that I didn't have a boyfriend and I was pissed off that he had a girlfriend. But in due time, he promised that she would be history. To make things right between us, we made a pact that tonight would be our fourth encounter. By showing up at his game tonight, we were going to make it happen. Win or lose, he wanted to be with me and I needed to be with him.

The lady in me took the stage to perfect our liaison. Dare I say that watching him was like visual foreplay without the physical touch. Focusing in on the game, I began to watch Derrick on the court. What turned me on about him was that he was an unselfish leader. I was also riveted by his gaudy confidence and physical stature.

Women young and old chatted incessantly about him. I was convinced everyone wanted him, but for the moment he seemed to be very interested in me. I, of course, was very interested in every inch of him.

I rose every morning to a varsity photo I clipped of him from the Essex Chronicle's high school sports section. I replaced his face on civil rights leaders, top models in magazines and evening news anchors. I smelled him, yearned for him and devoured chocolate in his honor. I adored his look and craved his touch. I even dubbed myself his number one fan in my full-length mirror.

Cheering for Derrick in a quiet frenzy, I watched him leap, shoot and rebound the basketball. Suddenly, the announcer blared into the crowd through the speakers. He stretched out his name to emphasize his greatness.

"Derrrrrrick Johnson has the ball.... ohhh, fake spin on number fifteen, nice release.... he scores! Derrick Johnson hits the two and draws the foul bringing the game within two points!"

The crowd rocked and swayed like a school of fish in unison. They slapped each other's hands and shook their pom poms along with the cheerleaders. The crowd rallied in and chanted, "Sink it, hands up! Sink it, sink it, hands up!" Opposing cowbells rang out to throw off his concentration. My chocolate honey wasn't phased by the noise as he positioned the ball for his foul shot. Time stood still as he extended his right leg and leaned forward. His masculine hands cupped the basketball as I dreamed of him cupping me like that. He positioned his shot straight up as the announcer's voice blasted through the speakers again.

"Derrick Johnson is at the foul line, it's up, and it's in!"

The crowd jumped up and down in complete pandemonium. Derrick received the ball and parlayed his shot into position. The crowd was silenced by his concentration and the thrill of possibly tying the game. The crackle of the speaker's voice heightened our suspense.

"All eyes on DJ, it's up, it's in! DJ is sending this game into overtime!"

It was simply too much for my heart to take, so I sat down to catch my breath. But the drum section forced everyone back on their feet to a thunderous applause. Even though Derrick was sweating profusely, he remained poised and in control.

Proud and confident, my baby ran to the sidelines with the rest of the team for a twenty-second time out. Waiting for them was the king of the high school coaching world, the Irish pit bull, Coach Mahoney, or to the insiders, "Maniac Mahoney." He loved St. James, high school basketball and all of his players. Mahoney was like a second father to the players. For some, their only father. Coach Mahoney shoved his finger into each player's face. He wanted and demanded their undivided attention. This was an important game in his thirty-third year as a coach. His loud raspy voice blasted into the team as the entire crowd read his lips.

"Come on guys! I want this to be a smart game. Mookie, no fouls, dammit, we need you! Keep those hands straight up and no fucking fouls! I want all eyes on Ricky! Rick, stay posted at the top of the key, for all the hot-dogging you do in practice, I want a three pointer! You hit that shot a million fucking times in practice, so focus on the three and get your damn rebound if you miss! I want a one on one full court press on defense." He pointed at Derrick and said, "Make sure you don't let number fifteen out of your sight! He left a shit load of diarrhea in our toilets and he's playing like Julius Irving. If you lose tonight, each one of you is getting a crack at cleaning that toilet bowl out! Let's go boys, get at em' and win this damn game. Ready...fists together boys, fight, fight, fight St. James!"

The foghorn blasted and it was time to resume the game. Pity though, it seemed like the excitement was too much for them. St. James lost, double overtime and by two points. The final buzzer seemed to blare through the gym for hours as the disappointed students and parents stood motionless. Some gripped their leather gloves. Danny gnashed his false teeth and some spectators stood in shock, holding their heads in disbelief. Maniac Mahoney shook hands with the opposing coach and stormed off the court swearing all the way through the locker room doors with his white hair sticking straight up. The season wasn't over and there was going to be hell to pay in practice.

Despite the loss and fat chunks of snow falling outside, I was determined to be with him just like we planned. I looked at my watch and thought, "Damn, it's 9:30 pm already, thirty minutes shy of my weeknight curfew. Fuck it. I'll tell them I was at the library." I had to take my chances tonight. He's certainly worth the risk.

Derrick palmed the basketball with one hand and slammed it into his other hand as he gave Mookie a pep talk. Then he threw the ball to the referee barely missing the point guard from St. Thomas High School. For one quick moment, he looked up at the top of the rafters and spotted me. The hairs on the back of my neck rose. I gave him that, "I'm so sorry you lost," smile, and with that he turned around and headed straight for the locker room. Great! At least we made eye contact and he knows I'm here for him in every lust filled way. Hopefully he'll take a quick shower but forget to rinse around the base of his neck. I like a little left over sweat on my man. I could only imagine how nuzzling in his neck through his varsity jacket would turn my pink panties into sweeter creamy silk.

Damn, 9:51 pm, still waiting. It takes a while waiting for a B-ball player like Derrick. He was tight with the entire team. Especially the Brat Pack; Ricky, the Pretty Point Guard, Damon, the Small Forward, Darren the Demon Power Forward and Mookie the Dumb Ass Center. One good thing going my way was that the gym was clearing out fast, parents, scouts, horny groupies and all. The snowstorm prediction was right on target, dropping a half an inch per hour. By the time Derrick made it to the lobby with the fellas, the only remnants of tonight's defeat were sticky gum wrappers, wilted pom pom strings and Gus the maintenance man. I quickly turned my back on Derrick, leaning against the windowpane pretending to wait for a ride that would never come. Even though no one else knew about our rendezvous, I had to make it look good for the guys. Dumb ass Mookie called me out first.

"Yo, Yo, ain't that Shanelle right there?"

In sheer disgust I said to myself, "Damn, I don't want Mookie to look at me, let alone ask me for a ride home, but he's going to ask me with his retarded ass."

Don't get me wrong, Mookie is a nice guy, but he's also a weed smoking illiterate who spent his entire education being socially promoted because he could play basketball. No one gave a damn. Everyone spoke openly about how dumb he was, but bragged about the skills he possessed on the basketball court. The Essex's Chronicle wrote frequently about Mookie's lack of intellect, while the school openly chose to ignore it. Mookie filled the gym to capacity crowds that spilled out the campus doors and onto the sidewalk. He was well on his way to accepting a coveted college scholarship with a division one school. For now, if you got in his car for a ride, he would light up a spliff, smoke it with the windows rolled up tight and then stop at the Number One Chinese Spot for three quarts of beef fried rice. He needed at least ten duck sauce packets to kill the craving. I wasn't interested in Mookie, his car, the Burger King wrappers on his front seat or his, "I be, um, she be, um," conversation. I needed to be with Derrick in the worst way. He seemed to know it too, because he walked right past Mookie and right behind me. The wool on his varsity jacket brushed the back of my hand.

"Stay cool Shanelle," I thought to myself. Sure, I wanted to turn around, jump on him and wrap my big legs around his waist while he squeezed me tight. I wanted to pretend that St. James won the game, and that Derrick had four assists, eighteen points and no errors for the coach to throw in his face. As if the team had advanced to the finals, I wanted Derrick to carry me down the stairs, find a clean patch of snow with no footprints, blindfold me with his wool scarf and fall on top of me. The thought of Derrick sliding his thick warm tongue into my mouth enhanced my mini daydream. Just thinking about it caused Kitty to purr. Even though he was pressed up against me in the lobby, I was still stuck in my fantasy. My dream was intense and I needed to remember the things I had to say to him after all this time. The words I envisioned were simple. I would start by saying, "Derrick, I love you. Even though I never sent you a love letter, I know that I love you. There are so many memories of you in my head that I have to write them down to keep track. I passed you by in Dr. Jays and I could barely say hello. You were buying Chuck Taylor's in black and I in turn, spent my last fifteen dollars buying a pair in pink and laced them with black shoelaces. I strained my neck on the Hoodaville bus as you passed me by walking to school. My chances of seeing you are four to one. I have to leave my house one hour early just to have a chance encounter with you in the morning. I sing Chaka Khan's "Sweet Thang" to stay connected to your beautiful vision. I can't sing, but I don't care. People look at me like I'm crazy, but the old ladies who went through this shit back in the day know just what I'm talking about and they can feel my pain. The words come easy when I'm on the phone, but when I'm with you I'm like butter in the hot sun. When I come to your basketball games, I know my eyes say to you, 'Derrick, I love you, can I be your lady?"

Moving out of that sweet Love Jones, I looked directly into his eyes and came out of my trance. Derrick must have known I needed to say these things. He whispered to me, "Let's get outta here girl, the game is over and it's about you and me now."

I responded by taking his lead as he opened the lobby doors with his free hand. He took his other hand and placed it on the small of my back and led me out the door. My entire body felt sensationally warm like the fifteen minute after effect of sipping dad's cognac during the holidays. The warmth of his touch heightened my senses and aroused my nipples. I had a sexual energy about me that was seeping out of my pores and glistening my skin. Snow and wind swept in as the door opened into the night. Boisterous heckling followed us, but I was not disturbed, because tonight, he was all mine. One of the Brat packers belted out, “Yo man, you know you can only get booty from Nicky when we lose like this.”

Uproarious laughter ensued from the brat pack. Another one yelled. "I thought you were leaving with us D, or is tonight the night man? Haaaaaa! Haaaa!"

“Yo man, this is the third time this week you opened a door for a girl, I hope you get some booty wit dat!”

I recognized that voice as illiterate Mookie. His comment was so corny and he was the only one laughing. Derrick paid them no mind and put his arm around me as he led me down the snow trampled steps. Half of his scarf blew sideways into the fierce and steady wind. The fringes of his scarf brushed my nose and landed on my chest for a quick moment. The smell of Paco Roban overcame my nostrils along with the cold air. I was breathing heavily from the excitement of his strong touch. He spoke to me like we were the last two people on earth.

"Don't pay any attention to them, they're all crazy from the loss tonight and each one of them wishes they were me right now."

Taking in what he said, I honestly asked, "Why?"

He licked his big brown beautiful lips and grabbed my hand to strengthen the intensity in his answer.

"Because Shanelle, you're a lady, a beautiful lady and any guy would be crazy to let you out of his sight."

My chest was heaving under my coat. I bit the lower corner of my lip and put my head down, but he lifted it back up with his finger.

"Did you hear what I said Shanelle?" I quickly responded.

"Yes, I heard you Derrick," biting my lip again.

This time he responded to my nervous affection for him. It came with a soft kiss. It was so unexpected that I was not ready to receive him. But I accepted his kiss because it was long overdue. He pulled away slightly and we stared at each other with complete lust. He took his thumb and rested it on the base of my throat. He stroked it ever so slightly and used his other four fingers to stroke my neck. Then he leaned in and tongue kissed me for the very first time. His tongue tasted absolutely delicious as he made love to my mouth. He tasted like mint and citrus. Perhaps he ate a Starburst after he brushed his teeth. But the pleasure of his tongue for the first time slicked a layer of clear silk onto my panties. The corner of my eyes began to well up with tears as my face relaxed with pleasure. I moved in closer to him, placed my hand on his sculpted waist and slid my hand around his ass and up the center of his back. Surely I would never let him go. Taking in his scent and feeling the wool on his coat strengthened my longing for him. He felt wonderful against me, like a leather glove on a delicate hand. A ferocious beast fired up in his pants and spoke to Kitty.

"I want you young lioness."

My Kitty replied, "Raaaaaaarrrrr!"

Suddenly, a thunderous roar erupted from the lobby. Nothing seemed to matter to me because I was simply swept up in his kiss and the soft powdery flakes of snow melting on my face and neck.

Just then, something hard and cold hit me and broke up into cold dusty flakes. The sound startled me into consciousness. Poof! Poof! Poof! Three snowballs dead on target, hit me in the ear, on my neck and back. I turned around to take in the assault.

"Ugh!" I thought to myself. It was pain in the ass, Pretty Ricky. He had good aim in every sport he played, especially as a second baseman for the varsity baseball team. He was more than happy to breakup Derrick's joy since he wasn't getting any play from me. Ricky was a future sex offender who skillfully harassed my ass since grade school. He sickened me on sight and I hated when he was around

Derrick because it brought out the "boys will be boys," attitude.

Derrick suspended his Love Jones for the snowball fight. He rounded up a mound of snow in his hands and joined them in the fest. He shouted, "Let the games begin!"

I took pleasure in the fact that he was going to sweat some more under his coat after a fresh shower. Derrick threw a clean shot that popped dumb ass Mookie in his left eye. Mookie was furious, but I'm sure he would not be able to recount the incident if an accident report needed to be filled out. He yelled, "Damn man, stop playin!" He was so stupid he didn't have the sense to make a snowball; he just scooped up two armfuls of snow and started throwing it everywhere, which settled right back to the ground. PAP! Another snowball hit me in my right ear. I screamed at a high pitch, the kind that makes cats and dogs stand up and pay attention on a Saturday night. It may have been a girly scream, but I had a whole lot of tomboy in my back pocket. I yelled out into the exchange of firing snowballs, "That's it, it's on now!"

I rounded up one and hurled it at Mookie. My first attempt clocked him in the back of his big ass head. Funny, his head was flat in the back like he spent the first eight months of his life lying in a crib screaming for someone to bond with him. I likened him to having a mattress head. I fired another snowball at Ricky's Adam's apple. He damn near choked himself reacting to the busted snowball on his neck. I yelled out, "That's what you get for pulling my hair every day in the third grade you punk ass!"

Derrick quickly looked at Ricky and I. That was the first time he probably heard that me and Ricky went back to grammar school days. Although he was enjoying the romp, I knew that my baby wanted to quiet Ricky down and the rest of his crew. I stood helplessly ducking and dodging snow balls so Derrick could rescue lil' ole' helpless me. Derrick positioned himself in front of me as if to shield me from the playful attackers. He quickly turned around and grabbed my hand to run in the opposite direction.

Cutting into the cold wind, we ran past his Chrysler Lebaron, dodged the mini salt trucks and headed straight for lot number two. To get there, you have to scale a three-foot embankment and then slide down the other side. I was breathing so hard I could barely clear the wall. He pulled me up to the top of the embankment and we fell backwards into the snow and rolled down the hill. We were laughing hysterically as the snowdrift landed on top of us. Snow was everywhere; in my eyes, nostrils and belly button. My short sweater could barely tuck into my Gloria Vanderbilt jeans and the gray pea coat I was wearing could not shield me from the wind swept snow. I jumped up to brush the snow off my stomach. It was so cold, yet so exciting. Derrick laid in the snow propped up on his elbows watching me brush the snow off of my coat.

"Come here," he said, reaching out his hand for me.

"Where?" I said, as I bit my lip in girly delight.

"Girl, don't make me have to come after you."

"Please do," I said, as I took off running further into lot number two. I was a fast runner. Kicking my sprint into gear like the 440 relays, the tap of his fingertips hit me in the center of my back. I fell face first into the snow behind a white pick-up truck. He was barely breathing as he fell on top of me. The lion in his pants seemed longer and harder this time as he pressed his weight down on me. He took a deep breath and stared at me. His eyes spoke to me in a passionate and gentle voice. I knew no harm would come to me, trust was our first connector, rippled with blissful teen passion. He continued to stare at me, locking into my need for trust. He grabbed my hand and didn't let it go. I wasn't confused. I was captivated by his presence and the masculine feel of his body that covered my five-foot five frame.

Distant voices from the snowball fight drifted away, chained tires scraping the ice-slicked ground, echoed away into the distance. Rusting engines from salt trucks driving by suddenly disappeared.

Another kiss ensued and I was completely and physically his. Heavy petting filled my Freshman existence as we kissed behind that pick-up truck for what seemed like hours. The nape of his neck contained the sweat I was craving. I kissed him, caressed him, stroked his hair and called his name. He grinded me and molded me into a sculpted piece of art. I pretended there were no coats, hats and pants between us. My brain was gone, as rhyme and reason swayed back and forth. I was confused, but everything felt so good.

Floating above my steam clouds of lust rested "Ms. Nemesis." She was my daily guide and anti-lust coach. She sang a soft lullaby to me, "Virgin girl, oh virgin girl, where are you, virgin girl?" Oh yes, every good girl has one.

"Will you give yourself to Derrick, or send him home with blue balls?"

I blocked her out and sized up his back to gage our physical compatibility. My size ten frame and big thighs could support his thrust, pump and body weight. He used his right knee to spread my left leg and my eyes started rolling around in the back of my head. I thought to myself, "Damn, could it get any better than this?" I was breaking every morality code I learned about in grammar school. But why was I thinking about school and what I learned? Damn, I just want him now and I wish my mind would stop racing.

Derrick enhanced the feeling by saying, "Oh, Shanelle, you are simply beautiful."

I responded rhythmically saying, "You are everything that is beautiful." I closed my eyes hoping he understood my need for him and by the look in his eyes, he did. He was breathing with me and said, "Shanelle, I need to be with you now, you are everything I need and I need to be inside of you."

My breathing sped up with excitement. I lost focus with reality and whispered, "Then take me now Derrick."

He continued to kiss me and then paused. “No, I want you girl, damn, I want you, but not like this." He continued talking, this time nuzzling a whisper in my ear. "I want to take you to my room and make love to you girl for the very first time." He knew it was my first time because I told him on the phone during one of our late night conversations. Even if his plot for me was malicious, no court or jury would have sealed a conviction. He was as honest as they came for an eighty's boy. I looked at his face straining in pain, passion and confusion. We could have easily let the moment happen right there. The lion in his pants began to grind in my pelvic area as Derrick called out for me.

"Damn girl you feel so good, but I've got to get you to my bed, that's all I want right now."

I chimed in breathlessly, "Me too and I'm getting cold. Just tell me what to do and I'm yours."

His face strained like he needed to hear that from me. He kissed me again. It was gentle and warm. He slid his hand down my body and unbuttoned my coat. Derrick softly bit my left breast with just the right intensity. I arched my back and took in all the pleasure his touch created and released it onto my signature pink panties. He slid his hand over every inch of my frame. He shook his head and said, "Damn girl, look at you, you're absolutely beautiful from head to toe." He seemed to gather his senses by pausing first, taking in a deep breath and then stood up. He lifted my entire frame from off the ground like a corny ass soap opera.

"Let's put this on pause for now."

I started to giggle as I grabbed his scarf for an extra grip.

"Am I a chocolate snack?"

He laughed as he gently put me down.

"No, you're a whole lot more than that Shanelle."

I loved it when he called my name. He made me feel special and wanted. We talked on the phone about the things we would do that would make me feel even more special like buying cotton candy and winning a stuffed animal for me at the local carnival. I couldn't wait to get my hands on a big blue Smurf. He was the only one that took the time to say my name like my name had real meaning. More importantly, even in the throws of hot passion, I was a lady to him.

Derrick kissed me again like he was so glad I was with him. My hair was drenched, and the wool fibers on my coat pierced my neck, back and stomach. I stopped his kiss and grabbed his face to look at him. I couldn't believe this was not a dream. He was patient. He stared back and said, "What is it Shanelle?"

My mouth opened but nothing came out. He kissed my neck and bit at my earlobe and whispered, "Tell me girl, you're driving me crazy."

I couldn't speak the words I practiced over and over again. I stuttered, "Der, Derri... are you for real? I think about you all the time and I can't believe we're here right now."

He responded by squeezing me tight. "Believe me, I want you so much girl... damn, you don't even know... but if you give yourself to me, let's make it special. I want us to remember this moment for a million years."

He squeezed me tight again, sensing that I was getting cold. Even if frostbite set in, three or four sawed off toes would not have mattered. I was lost in his warm embrace. I looked up at the black sky gazing at sparkling stars unknown. My favorite song began to play from a distant dorm room. It temporarily diminished my confusion. My heartbeat began to slow down as I focused in on the song... ***Sometimes in the night, I call your name...*** I finished the song in my mind as I surrendered to his touch. All I could think was, "That song is the bomb!"

The melody caused Derrick to surrender to me as he started to kiss me again. We fell back into the snow with him on top of me. He used one hand to elevate my head and used the other hand to skillfully slide it right into my creamy panties. Since he was taller than me, it was easy to get access to Kitty. My jeans were very tight, but the running and romp in the snow loosened the waistband and made it easier to get to her. I slowed his pace down without offering specific instructions.

"Derrick, I don't want this night to end... you feel so good, but please, I don't want it to be like this."

Derrick respected my nature and pulled his hand away. He picked up some snow and rubbed my nectar into a delectable miniature snowball. I stared at him with wide curious eyes as he smiled and then popped it in his mouth like a chocolate bon bon. He rolled it around with his tongue and took in the taste.

"I need to get my own ice cream made out of you. You are simply delicious."

I was in awe of his sexual creativity.

I looked him straight in the eyes and said, "It's all yours, the ice cream, brown sugar and whatever else you want it to be."

He stood up and helped me off the ground for the last time. He took off his varsity jacket and put it around my shoulders for warmth. Shielding me from the cruel temperatures, Derrick said, "I'm glad to hear that, so let's go back to my car and..."

My quick thought process interrupted him.

"Dammit, what time is it?" Derrick checked his watch and said, "12:15, why?"

His answer made me stomp my foot as I replied, "Shoot! My mother is going to kill me, that's why."

Derrick pulled me close to him and replied, "Well there's no sense in rushing, you're late anyway, let me get you dry, warmed up and then I'll take you home. Call your mom and tell her I'm going to drop you off, you know your mom loves me."

My mother, loving Derrick? Oh hell yeah she did. Any man with good hair, a 3.9 GPA and heading to Cornell Medical School, after a four-year Duke University undergrad tour, was a knight in shining armor. Just last week he spotted us at Shoprite struggling with a month's worth of groceries. He pulled up next to our car, placed the groceries in the trunk and left my mom gagging and bragging about Derrick for four days straight.

Derrick held my hand as we walked back to the gym to call my mother. He tried to assure me that I wouldn't get in trouble for my curfew violation. He was wrong. There would be hell to pay and half of it unrelated to the curfew. Gus let us back into the vacant gym to call my mother. Her high-pitched voice blasted through the earpiece of the pay phone and bounced off of every wall in the vacant gym.

"Get your ass home now Shanelle, and when your Father and I get through with you, you're going to have to buy another ironing board because I'm going to break this one over your goddamn back."

Oh brother, another violent threat. Mrs. Viv loved to threaten me, but the threats were always impossible to carry out.

"Don't you get smart with me girl, I'll shove this iron down your throat." "You better lower that tone Missy before I put my foot up your ass." The list went on and on.

Even if Derrick had my back, this would be the big one. For the moment, I didn't care. On the way home, I smiled as I relaxed in the pleasure of his touch. It would only take five minutes to get there, but the feeling was euphoric. The houses nestled on South Center Street looked like ginger bread houses dipped in white frosting. Tree branches bearing the weight of the season crackled under the weight of the snow.

There was silence in the air that pierced the night. Cars drove by slowly just to admire the scenery. Derrick pulled me closer to him as we enjoyed the snail pace home. His car was lit up with the scent of a brand new vanilla tree freshener. With the heat on full blast, it quieted our senses and forced us into silence.

Derrick turned the corner and pulled up in front of my house. We kissed goodnight one last time as my heart began to beat rapidly. Fear and anxiety seeped into my blood stream. Out of sheer nervousness, my eyes shifted to the front window. Since our phone was back in service, I wrote my phone number down on a small piece of paper praying that the phone had not been cut off again. Out of frustration for the unknown, I slid closer to him and buried my face in his neck.

"Is it that bad in there?" Derrick asked. I wanted to lie like Penny from Good Times. Watching Penny on TV was a great escape. I felt like I wasn't the only one with fucked up secrets.

"Yeah, it is, sometimes."

It was past my curfew and too late to describe my version of the trilogy of terror on the third floor, so I kept quiet. Derrick said in a quiet tone, "Why don't you just come home with me? My mom works nights and doesn't get home until eight o'clock in the morning."

It was a comforting gesture and I didn't realize that tears were flowing down my cheek and neck. There must have been sheer desperation in my eyes because this was not part of our plans. Derrick wiped my tears away with his basketball towel which left his scent all over me again. It gave me the strength to slide back over to the passenger side.

"I'll call you if I need you."

Derrick put the car in drive and replied, "Baby, I hope you don't need me, but I'll be here if you do."

I got out of the car and headed up the walkway. Twenty paces was all needed to meet my punishment. Mrs. Viv was ready for me because the vertical blind swayed back and forth revealing a glimpse of her yellow terry cloth house coat. I turned around and waved goodbye to Derrick. I used the storm door to clear a path to the main door. A mental pause froze my hand.

What will happen to me tonight? Should I run now or face the consequences?. Will evil be waiting for me on the second floor? I knew that I was in trouble and I could not wish it away. At a minimum, I could expect a suburban curse fest with a few jabs to the head.

Ding, ding, ding, in this corner, weighing in at one hundred and thirty-five at five foot five inches, Shanelle Brown. In this corner, weighing in at two hundred and forty pounds, Mrs. Vivian Brown. The fight began the minute I opened the door.

"What the hell is wrong with you girl?"

Pap! A back handed blow to the head. I was barely through the second door to notice that I was flying into the key rack. I took two steps forward to avoid another backhand when Mrs. Viv yelled, "Don't you walk away from me, get your ass over here."

Dear Daddy had a front row seat in his favorite burgundy crushed velvet chair. The enforcer held his cigarette between his pointer and middle finger taking in the fight. The embers moved upward in a slow consistent pace to compliment the enforcer.

"Didn't I tell you to bring your ass straight home from school?"

Push! A firm right hand to the collarbone knocked me into the bubbled unfinished wall. I began to mentally float away.

Fade to black Shanelle; think about how wonderful Derrick felt up against you in the snow. Take in the hits and laugh. It will be over before you know it. Let her win, she loves to be right, she loves to be in control.

I turned around to face Mrs. Viv and said, "I'm sorry mom, I was with Der," Smack! I couldn't finish my sentence without another smack in the face.

"I forgot to tell you about the game." Smack!

"Don't you lie to me girl. I'm not playing with you and neither is your father. Take your ass to bed before I slap the shit out of you for lying."

There she goes again, slapping the shit out of me. To think, there's no toilet tissue downstairs to clean up the shit when she gets finished.

I started walking up the old creaky staircase. My face felt raw and achy. The smell of snow, sweat, cologne and cigarettes in my damp hair began to clog my nasal passage. The first stair squeaked in the voice of a crumpled old witch. Who knew if evil had gone to bed? I didn't feel like being bothered. He was surely listening to the boxing match and loved the negative attention I received from Mrs. Viv.

I think I got smacked and cursed at so much because my drug crazed brother held my house mentally and physically hostage for almost one year now. Dear mother and father were so frustrated with him that they took their frustrations out on my minor infractions. He was in and out of the hospital for drug treatment more times than I can recall. He ate, slept, dined and passed his bowels with the richest druggies in Essex County's drug rehabilitation center. Movie stars and singers graced his neighboring hospital room. He bragged about it every time he came out, even the times he escaped. When he escaped, at least six police officers had to be called to the house to escort him back to the hospital. Detective Jackson always took the time to console dear mother when he went back.

"It's for the best Mrs. Brown, you've done the best that you can do with him as a mother, he'll only end up killing you and Shanelle if he stays."

Kill? Oh that's an understatement. That mother fucker would slice your ass in a minute if you didn't lock yourself in your room with a skeleton key during a full moon. Weed mixed with angel dust was too much for him after his football injury in 1978. His poor brain must have short circuited when he took that hit from the opposing linebacker. His helmet flew east and blood rippled from the crack in his skull at the base of his cerebellum. A team of specialists told Mrs. Viv that dear brother would be fine as long as he continued to take his prescribed medicines and avoid the use of marijuana. The strain of sitting on the sidelines and watching his friends soak up the glory during that championship year sent him into a binge of drugging and drinking. The chemical substances seemed to affect his brain in the worst way. He turned into a classic schizoid case and on any given day chased me and Mrs. Vivian up and down the creaky stairs, shut the power off in the house, blasted Richard Pryor records, and smeared his own feces on the attic walls. He adorned his room with pictures he stole from my photo album. All of my good friends were plastered into the dried shit like a fecal photo gallery. There was Candy, in her black two-piece bikini at Coney Island. Sexy Bonnie wearing her grape flavored lip-gloss in the 4x6 head shot I took of her in front of Upsala College. None of us could control his unusual behavior, nor dare enter his room. He took pleasure in the evening news, especially homicide cases in New York and 1980 was the perfect year for sensational coverage of famous celebrities. He wore Chuck Taylors and blue jeans with two scullys fitted together like a two-tone hat. That crazy fuck walked everywhere too and stayed in the best shape ever.

I found it difficult to wish him well. I could not relate to him or express empathy. He teased me constantly about my weight. He said I reminded him of a fullback from the Pittsburgh Steelers. I hated my body because of his cruel verbiage. Needless to say, if my own brother felt that way about me, what must other people think?

When things got really bad with his violent rages and Mrs. Viv needed a break, she would change the locks and throw him out for a week or two to fend for himself. While she was at work, dear brother would knock on the kitchen window like a Gino's drive through for two mayonnaise sandwiches before my father got home. The two things he feared the most were my father and the police. He suffered so much harassment as a school age child from the police that he was simply scared of them as a young adult. After twenty-three years of marriage, the only acceptable bad habit that could legitimately take up residence in our house was dad's cigarettes. He told Mrs. Vivian on a cold day in January that it was either their son or him. The vows they took prevailed and Mrs. Vivian kicked dear brother out in the blistering cold escorted by the North Orange Police. But before he left, the demon that ravaged his brain burned emotional scars into my mind that I shall never forget.

I took another step up and he started to laugh. Each step became increasingly sadistic. It was the sound of tapping metal to wood. The small taps became increasingly consistent and obsessive. It was part of his calling card and you had to accept it as his personal accessory. It didn't make sense to call on Mrs. Viv or Dad. They couldn't control him and his evil ways. As I reached the top landing and faced my bedroom door. Dear brother was waiting for me. He stopped the tapping temporarily to get my attention.

"Hey bitch, got any money?" Steven was sitting on the third hallway step leading to the attic with a butcher knife in his right hand spinning it into the step. This wasn't your ordinary sibling spat. This was psychological warfare with a twist of demonic humor. I turned to face him and said, "Not tonight, leave me alone and go to bed."

What I said had little effect. Steven was a tactical athlete and a drug head. The two combined enticed his terror strategy. Steven held his knife up and pointed it at my bedroom. I reacted by turning around. My door was slightly ajar. Steven quickly mimicked my response in a high pitched voice, "Not tonight, not tonight. Yeah well, you left your door open bitch. You better buy a new coat with that weak ass pocket change you get babysitting pee pee boy across the street."

Yeah, he was cruel, even when it came to innocent and mildly disabled children. But for the moment, I was consumed with the thought of possibly leaving my door unlocked. Maybe he was lying this time and I was spared from his get high thievery. I walked to the closet and pushed back my genie pants, but there was no leather coat. I pushed my black Jordache jeans out the way and there was no coat. I started to get warm inside. My throat began to clog with saliva. I could hear Steven jabbing the knife into the steps as he read my mind. The last push revealed an empty coat hanger.

"Go ahead and cry you fucking baby, I got some good money for that shit." He started humming a Jimmy Hendrix tune and ascended into the demon filled attic with his untouchable stolen treasures and erotic filth. Sure I cried, I had no choice, the release felt good to me as I cursed myself for being so stupid. I washed off my mascara, jumped into the shower and released my tears into the hot stream. The screeching sound in the shower pipes muffled my wail. That old pipe and showerhead muffled my cries for years. I always bathe slowly to wash away the sins of the day. The ones I committed and the ones committed by my brother against me. By now, the tears would have stopped but they didn't. I got out the shower, toweled off and donned my gray sweat suit. As I pulled the top over my head, I thought to myself, "I need Derrick. I need his touch, his warmth and his undivided attention."

I put some Visine in my eyes to reduce the redness as I dialed his number with one hand. The sound of his voice released a bellowing ache from my womb.

"Yeah, yeah, hello." He sounded disoriented, but woke right up when he detected my voice.

"Shanelle, what's wrong?"

"I need you now, please come pick me up now."

Derrick sounded nervous as he spoke with more clarity into the mouthpiece.

"Sure baby, hold on, I'll be right there, meet me down stairs in fifteen minutes."

I quietly hung up the phone and threw some clothes in my favorite duffel bag. All of my toiletries stayed in my room because dear brother loved to masturbate with scented soaps or wipe his ass with my toothbrush. I slipped past my parents' room and headed downstairs. Dear brother was directly behind me in a calm and calculated tow.

"Hey whore, you on night patrol?" He continued to taunt me with the knife and his questions.

"What time is pretty boy picking you up?" He pressed the knife into his pointer finger and said, "I bet he's light skinned, you love those Shalimar looking mother fuckers."

I laughed a little this time, shaking my head in slight fear and frustration. I thought to myself, "No you crazy fuck, Derrick's not light skinned, but let's focus on you. You're always on night patrol, slithering past our rooms and skipping the creaky stairs to get to the first floor."

Think it, yes, but if I expressed his psychotic behavior, the cool steel blade would have pressed against my neck with smooth precision. Steven skipped the stairs so much he wore out the side floor moldings three times. The banister came off the hinge and the opposite wall supporting his downward flight exposed his sneaky compulsion. Mrs. Viv got to work out her maternal codependency by wiping down the walls with Mr. Clean humming Sunday gospel tunes. The Clark Sister's rocked her in the bosom of Abraham and lulled her into a quiet existence. As she cleaned the walls, Mrs. Viv rhythmically clapped in rejoice of sweet redemption, "I'm climbing up, on the rough side of the mountain, I'm doing my best to make it in."

Satire ruled me as I listened to her singing, "No momma, dear brother is going to get you up the mountain and push you over the cliff if you don't get him out of this house."

But since I had to put up with him until Derrick came, I picked up my duffel bag and stood in the vestibule. He invaded my space and jabbed me in the back of my head with his pointer finger.

"Run along now bitch, goodbye."

The strain from his constant pursuit and mental aggression was all I could take for one night. I opened the front door and stood outside in the blistering cold. Once there was a barrier between us, dear brother was fine. I embraced the cold in order to escape his menacing ways. But at the same time, I cursed winter's serenity. It was forced upon me in the night without recourse or justification.

Steven locked the peeling white door behind me and put the chain lock on while he laughed victoriously. There was no rhyme or reason in waking up my poor mother. She was fast asleep, escaping her horrific reality. I turned around to face him one last time. His eyebrows grimaced in the window as he smiled. His mind was working up more terror as his breath forced hot steam clouds on the small windowpane. He slid his nose up and down and made piggy faces at me. Sometimes there was comedy in his routine when the threat was diminished. I thought to myself, "Oh God, it’s 2:00 am in the morning and I'm dealing with this crazy shit."

Suddenly, white lights turned the corner in the distance. It was Derrick and when he pulled up, the disease of my house whispered away.

Quiet Respite

South Orange kept up with the street snow removal throughout the early morning so we got back to Derrick's house quick. His house was warm and cozy. His God-fearing mother cooked a golden apple pie and left it sitting on the table next to her open leather bible. The Book of Corinthians seemed to be her resting place before she went to work. I wanted to be Mary Magdalene for Derrick, but I was too emotionally drained. Anyway, Derrick kept me morally sound. There was no offer to go to his room, even though I was curious. He led me into the living room, where a temporary bed was waiting for me. Derrick looked at me and said, "I didn't know if you brought pajamas, so I took out one of my tee shirts."

There were pajamas in my duffel bag, but his tee shirt was calling my name. He handed it to me and turned around so I could change. I peeled out of my clothes and let the warmth of his mother's house soothed my nerves. As I put on his tee shirt, the smell of fabric softener and Derrick's natural scent settled into my skin. Sensing my calm, he turned around and sat on the couch. With one leg resting on the floor, he pulled me down and pressed me against his chest. He felt warm and inviting as I relaxed into his breathing pattern. Then he took a comforter and wrapped me up in his quiet intensity. With him, I felt safe and warm. In my crazy existence, it didn't get much better than that.

Derrick woke up at 5:00 am and prepared egg whites and beef bacon. He was so meticulous about everything. Ironing clothes, cleaning up and washing his hands seemed routine to him. I knew he was the perfect catch to any girl who knew him. He woke me up at 6:30 am, laid out fresh linens and ironed my uniform. There was nothing left to do but to get pretty for him. I grabbed my duffel bag and went into the bathroom. The bathroom mirror was beautiful. It was oval with a beveled edge. I applied light foundation, soft pink eye shadow and of course, my signature mascara. Derrick liked "the natural look." He loved to stroke my face and smooth out the fine baby hairs around the base of my hairline. I applied pink matte lipstick, hot curled my hair and gave my face a final approval, which was a soft wink. My uniform was a dark-brown polyester single-breasted jacket and skirt. The skirt had two bellowed pleats in the front with a four inch hem. My skirt certainly teased the senses of a few good men, young and old. I had powerful thighs that were muscular above the knee and feminine in the calf. I wore brown socks that looked like sheer stockings. My signature hiding piece was a thin silver link chain. I kept it hooked from my signature satin pink panties to the inside of my skirt hem. I took that shit out after school so the chain could be exposed like the extension of a chastity belt. The fellas in the city loved that shit and cat called me everywhere I went. Oh, I had the freak in me, but nobody was going to get a taste. Well, maybe Derrick if he played his cards right. Confident in my final appearance, I went downstairs to eat breakfast. Derrick said I looked beautiful and gave me a warm kiss on my forehead. Since he was taller than me, I grabbed his wrist so his lips could stay there a little longer. He responded by shaking his body all over like he was shivering.

“Damn girl, let's eat before I get a boner.”

I wanted him to know what I was thinking so I replied, "I was hoping you already had one."

"Cute, Shanelle, real cute," he replied. But I knew he enjoyed my flirtatious ways. Derrick stared at me as he grabbed a napkin from the holder. He wiped my lipstick off and tongue kissed the hell out of me. One thing that got me going was his persistent need to spread my legs with his knee while we were kissing. I guess he loved being connected to the box as often as he could, waiting for the day to release himself inside of me. He backed me into the cabinet and lifted me up on top of the counter top. Derrick's wandering hands surveyed every inch of me, especially my inner thighs. If he wanted me, it could have happened right there because the feeling was so powerful. I was amazed that his face was filled with so much pleasure and that I was the one providing this early morning need. He buried his head in my aroused chest and let out a muffled wail, "Girl, you're driving me crazy!"

I grabbed his face and kissed him one last time and then I jumped off the counter top. When I landed, there should have been a bucket under my legs to hold the pleasure I released for him. With a silly grin on my face, I sat at the table and crossed my legs in sheer delight.

Like the happy little couple playing house, we ate breakfast and chatted about Blondie, The Police and Michael Jackson. I graciously washed the dishes and Derrick drove me to school. There were breaks of silence on the way to school that were reflective and dismissive. Perhaps Derrick was thinking about what didn't happen last night. I, on the other hand, was thinking about that chick named Portia. I couldn't figure out what was on Derrick's mind, but I knew something was bothering him.

He pulled into the parking lot, threw the car in park and put his hand on my knee. I leaned into him and rested my head on his shoulder. Curiosity forced the question, so I asked, "Derrick, what about Portia?" Derrick looked at me and grabbed my hand tight.

"I know, we need to get that straight, I've been thinking about it too."

Something interrupted his thought process because he got off the subject and said, "Listen, call me when you get home and let me know if you need a ride to basketball practice. When I ironed your clothes I noticed you didn't have your uniform for tonight's game."

Derrick never missed one of my games and that intensified my attraction to him. It also pissed me off because even though he followed me in the high school sport pages and went to my games, he was still messing around with that damn doe-eyed bitch Portia. My best friend Candy used to say that when Derrick was physically with Portia, he was yearning to be with the sexy point guard from Wayne Valley High. I wanted to get out of the car with a funky, "I hate you attitude," but that baby brown face was irresistible.

"So, not only do you want to get with me, you want to be my agent too?" He didn't think that was funny, but at least I got a kiss to get me through the day.

"Just call me later and we'll talk about everything tonight."

I gave him my big baby brown eyes and sang a cheerleader rally, "Ok, Derrick, Derrick, he's my man."

Leaving him with something to think about, I grabbed him by the face and slid my tongue into his mouth like a hardcore chick. It seemed to work because I kept my eyes open and watched his face get all twisted up with pleasure. I pulled away and he took me back into his mouth. I pulled away from him and nibbled on his ear ever so gently. He opened his legs and I caressed his loins. He called my name with obscenity mixed in, "Damn Shanelle, you don't know..."

I interrupted him and completed his sentence.

"I do know and I hope we can get it together." I wiped the residue off of his mouth and one of the punk rock Wayne Valley boys shouted, "Yo, get a room!"

We both laughed at his fake Rocky Balboa impression. It was also a good way to end our sexy interlude.

I got out of the car and walked across the school parking lot. I gave him a runway walk to remember me for the rest of the day.

Head held high, legs slightly bowed and a strut that made the back of my skirt bounce off my booty. He didn't pull off until my ass got into the damn building. I knew that walk gave him something to think about. As for me, Portia was on my mind and a plot was hatching in my brain about what I needed to do to kill that bitch.

Portia

As for Portia, she had Derrick below the waist for the past three years and that was the "stuff" that had to be straightened out. It wouldn't be long before Pretty Ricky started blabbing about the tongue kiss he saw after the game. He dropped a dime on us to one of his concubines at St. Clark's Academy. In less than twenty-four hours, Portia was straight up in Derrick's face.

She didn't love him like I did. She didn't know how to love and she wasn't interested. Six degrees of separation kept me involved in Portia's life on a regular basis. My best friend Candy was cool with Portia's first cousin Selena. Selena despised Portia because Portia slept with Selena's man last summer. To get back at Portia, Selena dropped a dime on Portia to Candy every time Selena's mother talked to Portia's mother. Portia's mother had an insatiable drunken interest in Portia's diary. Portia told her mother that she was interested in journalism and that the stories in her diary was for a book she was going to write. Portia's drunk ass mother believed her and told Selena's mother about Portia's future novel. We all knew the stories were about Portia's man-eater flights. Candy always said that Portia's mother got turned on by her daughter's journal entries. Portia loved to test drive her Kitty but she always used a condom. She believed that using condoms kept her pure enough to sample until a real man came along to get a taste of her walls.

Everyone was interested in Portia because she was a stuck up fly girl from Maplewood. Back then, only six percent of the town was African American. Upwardly mobile blacks trickled into Maplewood enticed by the commuter friendly neighborhood and top rated school system. Portia's father was a pediatrician and her mother was a stay at home functional alcoholic. Her mother entertained Portia's every whim, including swimming lessons, art lessons, tap, ballet and Suzuki method piano. Every material need was met, every emotional need denied. Her family lacked affection in the worst way and it manifested in Portia's adolescent and adult behavior. She looked for love in all the wrong places, showering herself with tennis bracelets and gaudy bamboo earrings. Everyone knew her. She drove a black IRoc - Z Camaro, which was rare for brown beauties in 1980. That car stayed clean and blazed out everywhere she went. Every Papi Chulo, B-boy, homeboy and fly guy turned to see that pretty brown face and detailed I-Roc. She took her Kitty to Livingston, Nutley, East Orange, West Orange, Belleville and back to Maplewood looking for her claim to fame. She loved to hook up with pimped out boys whose parents owned box seat Mets tickets, floor seats at the Garden and NCAA Final Four tickets. In her down time, Derrick was her steady because he was the local boy, who, along with Mookie, received plenty of press coverage. Portia knew that she was going to break it off with Derrick in early July. Since Derrick was committed to four years of college and then medical school, she was determined to divorce herself from any more medical drama. She could thank her father for that. Her father was so boring and controlling that it drove her into fits of systematic bulimic rages. She binged at every medical convention and awards dinner. At home the rages were worse, but manageable because she was on her own turf and felt in control. The time spent in her car was liberating to her. Her daily routine included fast cars, hot boys and quick sex between 2:30 pm and 6:00 pm. Rumor had it she liked it hard and quick because she didn't like sweat and tangled hair. She had long shoulder length hair with a part down the middle like Cher. She didn't care if her hair was in style or not. The fact that it was long and flowing from the drop top IRoc was all that mattered. I saw Portia everywhere and she was a constant reminder of everything I wanted, especially Derrick. I saw her at Union Market, North Orange Park, The Peppermint, Zanzibar, Sandwiches Unlimited and Persuasions. That bitch was everywhere. Oh, I was everywhere too, but barely noticeable with her in the room. Portia walked in on any set and every girl damn near dissolved into the wallpaper. She had a bump up in the beauty, body and auto accessory department. In order to keep myself sane, I mapped out the life of Portia on my own terms. That way I could write that bitch off instead of kicking her ass. Here's Portia's story:

By August, Portia would be on her way to the coveted Spellman College. She immediately joined an elite sorority based on skin color and her father's social status. Like a wild fiend, Portia screwed every Kappa male in her path. A train here or there came in handy when she was real horny. During March madness, Portia would go to a step show at Morehouse College and be blown away by Rashan slammin' down his mighty feet. Rashan had sexy dreads that fell and swooped in different directions as he tapped his cane to and fro chanting, "I'm the mighty mighty Sigma, BOOM! BOOM, you don't know it but I see ya!"

Rashan's look was popularized by his father's love of Bob Marley and Peter Tosh. He was one of the first non-Jamaicans to sport his look on campus and Portia the man-eater was riveted by his physical appeal.

Visually locked onto her target, Portia sized up his manly existence, pecan tan skin and persistent sweat. She envisioned herself unbuttoning the pants that hid his hard, long loins. In fact, forty minutes later, she was. Rashan spotted Portia coming in the door. He was skilled at visual multitasking; onion booty at three o'clock, my boy Diggs in the third row; honey in the black jeans I hit last night. But after seeing Portia, it stopped. The step show moved into the quad and by 11:00 pm, Portia and Rashan were hitting a spliff and talking about black conservatism. Rashan was just what Portia needed in her shallow ass life. A five-year EOF student from Prince Street in Newark who didn't give a fuck about anything except getting high and opening a barbershop back in his neighborhood. His thugged out body blazed through his frat gear. He peeled off Portia's clothes just when the munchies set in and he ate her Kitty to kingdom come. He didn't care about her long ass hair either. He put so many knots in it fucking her he had to cut three inches off with his professional scissors. She loved the new look and Rashan. Rashan took her back to roots unknown. Every other weekend, Rashan and Portia blazed out back to Jersey pumpin' Luther and Teena Marie up I-95. Portia's father flipped out at the mere site of Rashan and Portia's short hair. Her mother giggled under her drunken breath. She was happy for her daughter's new look and fifteen pound weight gain. Rashan didn't give a shit what either one of them thought because Portia was all his. There was no way daddy could give Portia what Rashan was giving her on the regular.

The Jersey weekends included banging the headboard on three day old sheets and going to the Irvington Beauty Supply. Rashan kept a steady supply of blades and cheap black doo rags for his special clients at Morehouse. They jetted to Cuts Above the Rest on Springfield and Clinton Avenue to earn enough for the Turnpike tolls and a lunch break at the Maryland House. Rashan's best friend from Quitman Street Elementary School was holdin' the shop down until Rashan graduated. Portia sat in the shop, read Essence magazine, picked up $5.00 dinners and swept the hairs off the floor for her man. In two years, Portia and Rashan would be married with two kids, Hasan and Nicole. Portia's ass was so sexed out, her fat ass size sixteen jeans looked good to her every *time she looked into a full length mirror. The memories of her father, Derrick and binging were long gone.*

Wayne Valley High

Wayne Valley High in North Orange, New Jersey was the shit back in the day. Walking into the hallway was like visualizing "the freaks come out at night," but in the daytime. The door shut behind me as I walked up the stairs. Raheem, better known as "Ralphie" was waiting at the top. Nobody knew whether he was Italian or Puerto Rican, but it didn't matter because Ralphie just knew his ass was black. Big ass gold chains and a brown Kango adorned the upper half of his skinny frame. He got his ass kicked every day for trying to front, but you had to admire Ralphie because he kept coming back for more.

"Yo,Yo, what's up Cha-Nelli-Nell?" as he grabbed his crotch.

I looked at him with my usual smile and said, "What's up with you Ralphie boy?"

Ralphie sucked his teeth in frustration and said, "Yo, I keep telling you my name is Raheem, Ralphie is my slave name."

He was so funny in an annoying way, but the ladies loved Ralphie. He took my duffle bag and escorted me to my locker.

"Yo, I saw the way you slammed your boy in the car. I hope you're saving the real stuff for me though."

He was starting to get on my nerves.

"Yeah, just for you." I replied. "Have you seen Candy?"

"Yeah, your crew is downstairs eatin' breakfast but yo, you better tell Candy to lay off those donuts, yo, her titties are big as hell yo!"

Ralphie was good at perpetuating a stereotype. He emphasized his sentences by throwing in the word "yo," every time he grabbed his nuts.

"Shut up, Raheem!" I took a playful swing at him but missed. He ducked and put his fists up to his face to defend himself stating, "That's right baby, Raheem's too quick for you, but I can take you down the long stretch as soon as you give me some of that poon poon."

"Ralphie, get outta here with your nasty self." Ralphie had a two joke limit with everybody because after that he just worked your nerves.

"I'll see you at lunch Cha Cha. Stay sweet baby, you know I'm just playin'."

"Yeah okay."

Ralphie took off down the hallway blending into the population. The bell rang for first period and I was in no rush to go to class. I reorganized my duffle bag, touched up my pink lips, took out my algebra books and headed for the cafeteria to meet up with my girls before class.

The cafeteria was lit up already; the jocks were ordering their hungry man breakfast and turning around to see where Candy was sitting. My girl had that effect on the entire football, basketball and baseball team. No matter the season, Candy's slim hips, big tits and pouty lips had the jocks talking about her on the regular. As for my personal opinion of Candy, she was a wild child. Miss Thing walked it, talked it and left you begging for more no matter what she did. She strutted amateur runways, set fashion trends and could fly out her face with ten different shades of eye shadow. We clicked instantly the first day we met. She liked my genie pants and I liked her bob haircut. We loved club music, plum lip stick, Teena Marie, double cheeseburgers and hot boys who could make us laugh from the bottom up. We had different taste in boys and men. Our rule of engagement was simple, "If he were ever my man, he can never be yours."

Candy liked them tall, pecan tan, chiseled face with a big dick. No matter the shade, I liked them stocky, broad shoulders, deadly smile and a cut jaw line.

I wasn't too interested in the piece. I was keeping it tight for Derrick and having him lay on top of me in the snow mound locked the Kitty down for him.

Candy was at the table sliding petite pieces of a brownie down her throat, carefully avoiding a lipstick smudge. At 9:00 am, Candy could eat whatever the hell she wanted. She was barely a size six and walked everywhere. Hanging out with her was good for me because at five feet five inches tall at one hundred and thirty-five pounds, I was always conscious of what I ate. Candy gave me my props all the time. She made me buy cut off tops, sweaters and sweatshirts. Or she would take my shit and cut it herself.

"Show your stomach off girl, guys love that shit."

It felt good to have a friend like her in my corner. Trust me, I knew I was cute, but it took a lot of work to maintain that frame.

Speaking of frames, my other girlfriend Bonnie had a face and body like a work of art. She was sitting next to Candy at the table surveying the eclectic crowd. Bonnie was the feisty half Hispanic, half Black girl. Her Puerto Rican father blessed her with the thickest long black hair imaginable. It didn't matter whether it was natural or permed, she had waves for days and the flair to fling it around. She had fiery eyes and thick eyebrows. The braces she wore in grammar school paid off in a major way and that smile drew guys into her web like a black widow spider. Bonnie's mind was always at work, like Portia's future husband Rashan. She always looked you in the eyes and in a flash her eyes were reading the lips of two new pieces of after school gossip.

"Look at Joey over there with his big ass head, I hope he can convince the dentist he brushed his teeth because I can smell his breath from here."

Bonnie was funny as hell.

"Damn, look at Jameel, that boy got the munchies like hell and it's only nine o'clock in the morning."

She saw a familiar face walking by and said, "Mieda Papi-Chulo, call me tomorrow, I got that stuff for you."

Eric, a sophomore point guard for the varsity team, gave a nod of approval and kept it moving. Bonnie could kick that Spanish lingo back and forth and kept some secrets for herself. That was cool with me because we all had a few good secrets that were important enough to hide. Bonnie knew we were trying to figure out whether she and Eric kicked it last week. Guys were attracted to her mysterious flavor, so they had to work real hard to get her attention.

The three of us together set it off everywhere we went. Even though there were plenty of catfights to watch on a daily basis, no one fucked with us when we were together. One girl tried to get up in Bonnie's face over some ugly boy that she would never give the time of day to, but Bonnie kicked her ass up and down the hallway just for asking. After that, drama stopped following us. I took the empty seat next to Candy and jumped into the conversation. Only the popular girls sat with us at our lunch table. We were a bunch of make up wearing chicks that had eye and lip application down pack. It didn't matter whether you were Black, White, Greek, Portuguese, Cuban, or Italian. If your ass was fly, you deserved to sit there. That table blew up with scents of Knowing, Escape, Safari and Fendi. Hair spray was a must for the Portuguese and Italian set. If someone lit a match, the whole school would have blown up from the chemicals we emitted.

When the bell rang, Fendi bags and key chains jingled and swayed as the clicks bid each other farewell. As usual, Bonnie, Candy and I said goodbye with the peace sign and a wink. We didn't leave because we needed to catch up on gossip.

"Shanelle," Bonnie said, "Don't even ask me if I'm coming to the game because my mother is pissed off about that shit with Andre."

"Damn," Candy said. "She's not over that shit yet, that was like three months ago."

Bonnie's mom would not allow her to do anything after school except come straight home and fire up the pots and pans to cook rice and beans. Bonnie had to do her dirt from 8:30 am until 2:30 pm and then turn into the good Catholic school girl.

"No, she's not over it yet and Poppy took my gold chains. I can't even go to Great Adventures."

"Damn Bonnie!" Candy replied. "You need to run away from them, fuck them gold chains, you know Andre will buy you some more."

Andre was Bonnie's man since the eight-grade. A mighty mouth entrepreneur, he sold gold, silver and egg rolls if you wanted one bad enough. He was on his way to the top, once he figured out what he really wanted to do with his life. In the meantime, he had Bonnie's back day and night.

"I'm cool Candy, just make sure you bring me back a teeshirt."

"Ok, just make sure you give me ten dollars so I can buy you one."

Candy had a smart-ass mouth, but she always got her point across with no regrets.

"What's up with you Shanelle, I called you last night and your mother hung up on me. You need to tell me when you want me to cover for you. She thinks I lie with a straight face and she couldn't even see me."

I shrugged my shoulders in disgust.

"Same old bullshit, Steven started smoking that shit again, harassing me, knife and all."

"What?" Candy replied

"Yeah, I booked up and went to Derrick's house."

"Did you give him any pussy yet?" Candy asked.

I sucked my teeth to prove a point. "Come on now, he's not ready for this yet."

Candy sucked her teeth back and said, "Girl, you've got that boy so strung out, he's gonna come in two seconds the minute you let him in."

"Shut up Candy," said Bonnie. "You know Ney - Ney is into that endless love shit!"

They both broke out into simultaneous laughter. Candy started to serenade Bonnie like Lionel Richie to Diana Ross. Candy grabbed Bonnie's face and mimicked him.

"Two hearts, two hearts that beat as one." Bonnie ended it with a joke singing, "I think I'm gonna come."

They laughed harder and gave each other a high five as I picked up my book bag and tray.

"Real funny assholes, you know I'm sensitive about that shit. Let me get my ass to class, I can't fuck up this quarter because the coach will definitely bench me."

They were still caught up in their comedic moment, so I left thinking about Derrick and wondering what he was doing right now. Sometimes they teamed up on me about my good girl nature, but I was willing to stand alone in the virginity department as long as necessary. Derrick needed to do a lot to peel the panties down. But the smile on my face stirred up another fantasy as I took my seat in algebra.

I'm alone with him upstairs in his room, its 3:15 pm and the After School Special is playing on his thirteen-inch TV. Soft rain is falling outside. The clouds outside cast a dark shadow over his bedroom. His room is adorned with football and basketball paraphernalia. Derrick and I are wrestling on the bed. He lets me pin him a few times because he likes to feel my weight on top of him. With a quick maneuver, he is now on top of me staring straight into my eyes.

"Damn girl, you are so beautiful."

His words fill me with life as I begin to breathe heavier and heavier. I can't form any words because my whole face is worked up into a passionate frenzy. My eyebrows connect and I bite my bottom lip. He releases one of my hands from captivity, places his thumb in my mouth and strokes it slowly and gently across my lips to relax my tension.

"Shah, Shah, baby. Don't be afraid, I'm not going to hurt you."

Off in the distance I could hear Mr. Crollin, reviewing logarithms. I'm damn near grinding in my seat on this fantasy. Ecstasy pains are throbbing my Kitty.

Derrick frees his other hand and caresses my face. He kisses my forehead, eyelashes, baby hair and left ear. Then he starts to grind me into the mattress. Oh my, my panties are drenched. He entices my nectar to my inner thighs and takes pleasure in spreading it around. He pauses, getting up from the bed while I lay there, wet and ready to get the Kitty banged out. How can it possibly hurt when I feel like an oil slick? Derrick closes the blinds to surrender to darkness, turns off the TV and slides along side of me. His piece is pulsating on my thigh and he encourages me to feel it by leading my hand up and down.

"Oh Shanelle, I want you baby so bad."

"I want you too."

He begins to remove my skirt off until the chain stopped his flow. Oh, the chain, it was hooked to my satin panties.

"Yank it off baby and take me now!"

He pops the chain, slides the panties down and pulls out that luxurious piece of manhood. My back is arched off the bed. He takes three goose down pillows and shoves them under my booty. Holding his piece in his hand he...

"Shanelle, can you write out the answer to the second equation on the board, the chalk is already there."

"Hell no!" Can't you see that Derrick is about to slam my pipe? Oh I hate you Mr. Crollin! There are people in this world who can truly fuck up a wet day dream.

I was conscious again, squeezing my thighs together to squash the passion that was buried there

"No, I can't write the answer, maybe yo momma would like to try!"

Loud uproarious laughter bellowed from the class. Raheem led the pack with his big mouth screaming, "Yo, good one NEY-NEY, your timing was the bomb!"

The look on Mr. Crollin's face suggested that he was ready for retirement. Our antics were forcing his decision to call the employee services.

"Hello, is this employee services?"

"Yes it is, may I help you?"

"Uh, yes, this is Mr. Crollin, from Wayne Valley High School.. I'm about to lose my fucking mind. These kids are animals you know and I've had just about all I can take for one human being."

"Ok sir, so are you saying you want to retire?"

"Yes, that is correct."

"We'll put the papers in the mail for you today."

"Thank you."

"You're quite welcome Mr. Crollin, have a nice day, uh, if that's at all possible."

Mr. Crollin gathered his senses and said, "Ralph, take your big mouth to the office with Shanelle and make sure you give them this demerit slip."

Raheem yelled back at him proclaiming his fake ancestry, "Yo, I told you for the last time Mr. Crollin, MY NAME IS RAHEEM!"

Mr. Crollin ripped the demerit strip from his little pad without looking up at either one of us. His days of compassion were over and all he needed to do was hold on until the last day of school or topple over from a heart attack.

"Yeah, whatever, go to the office now!"

We both looked at each other and laughed. There was no way in hell either one of us was going to the principal's office. It was already 11:30 am and the bell was about to ring for lunch. Raheem hit the back door to fire up a joint and I went to the library to prepare for my Spanish exam. I also needed to catch a nap before the game.

Night Vision

The game against St. Bridgette's was a bust. The senior point guard from St. Bitches, as we coined them, was on fire, knocking down twenty-two points, six assists and four rebounds. Derrick came to the game, but I could not enjoy his presence with such a heavy loss. The coach was on my back to stick and box her out, but her game was just too tight for me. I was distracted and tired from playing the house bounce. During half time I kept thinking that this would be a good night to get some sleep in my own bed. Little did I know that when the 2:30 pm bell rang, the demon was back at 122 Crescent reeking havoc unknown to mankind. Everything intimate and personal was sliced, cut, shredded and smeared. Years worth of jewelry, perfume, clothing and shoes were frantically shoved into a black garbage bag to sell to the highest bidder. The intense desire to get high ravaged his taste buds and demonic hands. He wanted me to know that he was there and violated every inch of my room. He tracked mud with his old boots. He brought our overweight German Shepard named Kiko into my room to romp on top of my bed with his favorite bone and tennis ball. It took five days to vacuum and air out the dander that festered my allergy and asthma attacks. He enticed Mrs. Vivian by calling her at the Pride House Community Center.

"Get home Leo the Lion before I burn your fucking house down."

Mrs. Viv knew this was one of his big rages because she could hear Kiko thrashing and barking in the background. After he hung up on her, he took every phone out of the wall and put it in his loot bag. Mrs. Viv had the sense to quietly call Detective Jackson from the office before she left. It was a twenty-minute drive up Central Avenue to South Harrison to South Center to Crescent. By the time Mrs. Viv got there in the Chrysler, three police officers were in position with their guns drawn. Two knives were placed on top of each other in the sign of the cross as a warning. By the time Mrs. Viv got there, Steven was long gone. He cut through North Orange Park like the black grinch, slipping and sliding through the thawed snow as he headed towards Oakwood Avenue. Arriving at the Garvey Street projects, our possessions were sold in fifteen minutes flat under the darkness of the broken courtyard lights. People peered from their apartment windows as new items transcended from the garbage bag. Some wished they were downstairs braving the cold to get a phone, a leather jacket or my gold watch. Dope man waited in the hallway of quad #1 waiting for Steven to make a purchase. He brought more than five ounces with some dust to mix it with. The high blazed his lungs and crystallized his brains for hours. It was enhanced with cars driving along Freeway Drive simultaneously playing Frankie Crocker's 8:00 pm exit song.

James Moody's infamous song transcended on all of us; Mrs. Viv in the front of the house with the storm door open for the police, and for me, emitting through my headphones to wind me down from that miserable loss. The demon zoned out after the first chorus, but he had enough conscious about him to plot new vengeance and domestic havoc, time would only tell.

My vision was clear during the bus ride home. I wanted to take a long hot shower and get some rest. I thought to myself, "There will be peace tonight," until I reached South Center Street and Crescent Avenue. Cherry Bomb lights lit up the block. There were three squad cars with two-armed officers accompanying each car. The neighbors had seen so much drama over the years, only two showed up this time. Mrs. Viv was out front pacing, looking up and down the block. She walked up to me trying to remain calm but her voice was quivering.

"Your father is packing a bag for you. Steven had another episode and the police are checking the area for him."

"Ma, I need to go up..."

"No!" She shouted, "Wait for your bag and..."

"I don't want any bags, I've got too many bags, and I'm tired of going here, there and everywhere! If he's not here, so what!" I gasped for air to fight back the tears.

"This is crazy, I didn't do anything wrong and everybody's dancing around for him, commit his ass and forget about him!"

Mrs. Viv looked right through me; her eyes were over my shoulder looking to see if he was coming. I searched her shifting eyes for an answer, but all I could see was desperation. I thought to myself, "Always looking and dodging, peeking and peering, this shit is ridiculous." All I wanted was one night of peaceful sleep. Night vision can be so deceptive to the weary and weak. My defenses were down and I was vulnerable. I ran past Mrs. Viv and bolted up the stairs. The landing was full of soot and wood shrapnel. Dear brother took a saw from the basement and ravaged each bedroom door to gain access to sellable items just to get high. The magnitude was unbearable. Poor daddy, he didn't know what to say.

"Don't worry baby, I'll buy you another necklace." I thought to myself, "I don't need a necklace. I need my bed. Grab your bag girl, the damage is too deep. Quick list, combat boots, leather belt, black boxers, crop tee shirt, maxi pads and Pamprin."

Dad handed me a twenty-dollar bill. I grabbed the money from his hand and said, "I'll be back Saturday night. No I'll call first, so make sure mommy buys a phone tomorrow."

I picked up my bags and descended down the creaky stairs one by one. Each step had a voice that called out to me; pain, sorrow, bitch, liar, thief, denial, anger, kill, run away. The last step was reality. They were so wrapped up in the crime scene, they didn't offer me a ride. I headed back to the Forty-Four Bus, transferred to the Ninety Grove at Central Avenue. I didn't pay when I got on the bus. Mr. Jenkins, a solid NJ transit employee, drove me to Penn Station on many a night.

"Hey girl, what mischief are you up to tonight?" The pistons from the bus was the signal to sit down.

"No mischief tonight Mr. Jenkins." I took the second seat and asked him to wake me up at Grove Street. The ride to Candy's house was quick. For once, the Ninety Grove didn't take five hours to show up from hell raising Irvington Bus terminal. Mr. Jenkins was kind enough to block the intersection at Central Avenue and Grove Street. He signaled the driver to let me get on board his bus and I thanked both drivers for their small act of kindness. I walked to Candy's house in five minutes. She was sitting on the porch.

"No questions asked girl, go take a shower and crash in the blue room." The blue room was my second home and offered sanctuary for me when I was down and out. I took a quick shower and fell asleep fast. Candy woke up early to ask her father for a ride to school. The minute I got in his car I was fast asleep.

I slept through first period, algebra and in the cafeteria. The principal announced during lunchtime that certain students would not be able to take their midterm exams. My parents rarely paid the tuition on time. I didn't care.

Besides, it only gave me more time to study. Raheem would tell me everything that was on each exam anyway. That resolve led me straight to the library for a three-hour snooze. After school, Candy and I took the bus home and planned the rest of the week.

"I'm going to skip practice tomorrow since there's no game this week. I need to hook up with Derrick, he's supposed to let me know what's up with him and Portia." Candy immediately snapped her fingers as if she suddenly remembered something and said, "Oh yeah, I forgot to tell you. He called last night but you were fast asleep."

My face was in shock as Candy continued talking.

"We put bits and pieces together of what probably happened at the house, so he said he would pick you up tonight."

"Damn Candy, you held out all day with all of that?"

"Oh now, you know you're my girl and I didn't want to make you love crazed all day. You slept through most of the day anyway.

"Now wake up and put on your pretty game face. Don't forget to lather up the Kitty, she may come in handy."

Candy took her pen out of her pocketbook and wrote my future married name.

"How does this sound? Shanelle Monet Johnson."

She raised her arm up like a scene from Romeo and Juliet and said, "Yes Derrick, I'll marry you my love joy."

"Quit it, Candy." I replied. Candy knew my limits, and she said, "Ok, ok, girl, I'll leave you alone."

The Test

Derrick arrived promptly at eight. I bolted down the stairs and barely said goodbye to my home slice. I jumped in the front seat and plastered his cheeks with three quick pecks.

"Hmmm, happy to see me huh?"

I got smart with him replying, "Not really, well...maybe a little."

I decided right then and there that I was going to start letting my guard down with Derrick. After weeks of supporting each other's basketball games and playing flirtatious games with each other, it was time to get down to business. Derrick put the car in drive and headed down the street. He looked at me with concern and said, "Are you hungry?"

I immediately responded and said, "No, I'm cool and I need to watch my weight."

"Why, you look fine Shanelle, don't start trippin' on that I'm too fat..."

I quickly covered his mouth and he responded by trying to bite my fingers off.

"Stop playing, I am kind of hungry. I'll watch my weight when you're not around. Take me to Burger King please."

"Ok," Derrick replied. He drove to Central Ave and turned into the Burger King parking lot. Looking at the meals on the menu screen made my stomach growl. I leaned over him and screamed into the microphone, "Yeah, let me get a Whopper with cheese off the broiler, no mayonnaise, no onions, cut in half!"

The scratchy voice came back over the intercom.

"Is that all?"

I belted out, "No, gimme a large onion ring, a small fry and a small vanilla shake. I also need extra ketchup, at least five!"

Derrick busted out laughing. "Damn girl, I need to rob a bank to pay for that order."

I whipped out the twenty dollars my dad gave me but he refused to take it. He replied, "Save it, you're going to need it when you take me out to dinner."

The last thing I wanted to do was to be "out" I needed to be in a house and Derrick needed to be "in" me. He paid for the order at the window and I said to him, "Derrick, I really don't want to go out tonight, I just want to be with you."

I gave him my puppy dog eyes and he melted right in front of me. He tucked some strands of my hair into place with his hands and said, "Ok, baby, have it your way."

"So I can have you my way just like my Whopper?"

He chuckled, "Yeah, hot off the broiler, but don't try to cut my ass in half."

"Oh you got jokes now huh?" Slight laughter followed.

"I got something." Derrick replied.

The irony of good jokes and food didn't last too long. We cruised back to his house with the radio turned down low. The drive would surely take us past my street if he went down South Center Street. I held the warm package on my lap dreading his sense of direction. The aroma of the French Fries distracted me for a little while and caused my stomach to growl. I fed Derrick three hot fries at Westmont and South Center Street. As the light turned green, my throat started welling up. Derrick slowed down as he passed Crescent Avenue. Whether he slowed down for sheer curiosity, or to give me a glance at the house was anyone's guess. Passing by, we both saw a patrol car parked in front of the house. I acted like I didn't see it, but my face and body slipped into numbness. He noticed the physical change in my demeanor and patted my lap with his hand. We barely said two words to each other until we reached his house. When we walked inside, there was a sweet baked smell that aroused my senses. Ms. Johnson left a pound cake on the table with a note sticking out from the bottom of the plate. The cake was golden brown mixed with crimson edges. It was the kind of cake that didn't need icing because the richness of a plain slice was all you needed. We took off our coats and Derrick took my bags upstairs. Before he got to the second step he stopped, turned around and said, "I hope you're staying for the weekend. My mom went to a fellowship convention in Philly and won't be back until Sunday night."

There was no need for him to mention his father. His parents divorced when he was three and he relocated to Southern California. I was slightly distracted, starving and confused about one squad car instead of the usual three. My response was quick.

"Yes, I'm staying. Can I wash my hands in the sink?"

He started up the rest of the stairs and said, "Sure, make yourself at home."

Once Derrick was temporarily out of sight, I washed my hands with lightening speed, dried my hands with the Burger King wrapper and tore into my Whopper, damn near devouring it whole. I had to remind myself to slow down because with three large bites down, Derrick would surely think I was a hog. I slowed down to savor the bites. He came back downstairs and picked up a banana out of the fruit bowl. He stared at me wide-eyed and said, "Are ya hungry?"

With a mouth full of food I said, "Stop playing!"

"Ok, enjoy your food, I'm going to let you eat in peace."

He started watering his mother's spider plants in the kitchen, which looked like a chore he was accustomed to doing all the time. He washed his hands, dried them and then cut me a piece of cake. I think I was caught up in an anxious eating frenzy. I ate the cake with my shake and it was heavenly... for a little while at least. After the last swallow, the squad car came into focus again and the food seemed to sit in my throat. I started to panic and needed to escape.

"Derrick, I made a pig of myself, can I use your shower?"

He started picking up my wrappers from Burger King and said, "Go ahead, you don't have to ask. I put some towels and a washcloth on my bed for you, the last room on the left."

On any other day, his answer would have sent me into the passion pit, but I knew that riding past my house awakened the anguish in my stomach.

I started up the stairs feeling the food slowly sour in my belly. There were no creaky noises but the voices were in my head.

"Die bitch die, die bitch die, slut, whore, bitch." The soured food crept back up my throat. The texture and movement felt like maggots feasting in warm bile. I spotted the bathroom and plunged my mouth into the toilet bowl. There was never a need to put my finger down my throat. Anguish and stress sat in the pit of my stomach like a power lifter, forcing food back up in times of stress. The vile hurled out of my mouth for an eternity. My stomach heaved and jerked until my eyes felt like they were going to pop. Relief finally came. The cold rim of the toilet bowl cooled my sweat tremors. My fingertips relaxed as I looked for some tissue. I wiped my mouth, stood up and stared into the beveled mirror. My eyes were dark and blood shot. I was ugly. Gray hairs and dark circles rested around my eyes. One tear escaped so quickly that I could not catch it. I started to take off my mascara to blame my hideous look on the make up. I turned to the shower and turned on the faucet. I let the water run and peeled off my clothes. I folded each piece up slowly and methodically, thinking where I would place them in my traveling duffel bag. The madness of worrying where I would sleep or wash next was paralyzing me. Stepping into the shower, the chill of cold water woke me up. I tried to talk to myself to settle the voices in my head.

"Stay cool Shanelle. He can't hurt you here, you're safe."

I turned the knob for hot water. The two temperatures merged and relaxed my aching muscles. I began to take slow deep breaths. Air began to swell my brain as the pressure forced me into a moan. It rose into my mouth as I began to sob, deep and steady. There were no creaky pipes to muffle the sound. The bellowing went straight to Derrick's ears and in seconds he was banging on the bathroom door. Panic ruled him, "Shanelle!" BANG! BANG! BANG!

"What's wrong?"

BANG! BANG! BANG!

"Shanelle, please don't cry baby, let me help you!"

His plea of help weakened me straight to the floor. He heard the thump of my palms hitting the basin tile, so he kicked in the door. He took his shoes off and stepped inside with all of his clothes on, picking my rag doll frame off the shower floor. Forcing his hands under my armpits, he spoke to me with his cheek against mine. The water confused my need for him, as he spoke calmly.

"Whatever it is, let me help you, please don't do this baby."

He grabbed my arm to rest on his shoulder; he took the other arm to do the same and said, "Grab me girl, hold me and don't let go. I love you, but you need to let me help you."

With that declaration, I was free to surrender to him. I relaxed my arms and wrapped them around his neck. I was afraid we were going to slip, but with one arm he held on to the peach tile wall and lifted us both out of the shower. He carried me to his bed soaking wet, not worrying about the trail he left behind. The towels he laid out for me was waiting for us. He was unselfish in his need to make everything right for me. Derrick toweled off every inch of my body with swirling circling motions. He poured some lotion in his hands and rubbed his hands to warm the creamy substance. Derrick applied the lotion to my arms and shoulders like a professional masseuse. There was no sexual awakening in me, just pure peace and tranquility. I started to drift off as Derrick massaged my scalp. As I drifted off into dream sleep, serenity became my refrain.

I was euphoric, somewhere in a meadow filled with daffodils. I looked down at pretty manicured feet with pink polish. I tip toed lightly while I walked, carefully avoiding the beautiful perennials. I extended my arms to let the sun glisten upon my skin. I looked at my pink fingernails and noticed an engagement ring beaming on my left hand. I looked up in disbelief grabbing the temples of my head. I felt organza and wiring shaped into flowers. I looked at my body and noticed a white beaded wedding gown adorning my small frame. I had a small waist. It was not restricted by a corset or a girdle. I breathed in and out; the air was light and fragranced with honey suckles. I continued to walk right into a beautiful cathedral church. Bells were ringing and inviting me. Walking bare foot up the stairs, the doors slowly opened to receive me. One hundred feet of white silk adorned my path with petals of pink roses. I walked by familiar faces, as they "oohed," and "ahhed" at my beauty.

"She's beautiful."

"Oh, her dress is divine."

"She is so special." A deeper toned voice bellowed out from a distant pew.

"Look at the whore bitch, she should have worn black."

My body flexed and hardened, but Derrick lulled me back into REM by rubbing the center of my back with downward strokes. *I continued down the aisle smiling back at the admiring guests. As I reached the end, Derrick was there to receive my hand. A minister was also present. He was tall and inviting. He announced with dignity, "Is there any person who objects to this sacred union?"*

Suddenly, there was a deadly and gothic response from the second pew. I turned with unanticipated horror towards the guests. I looked down at my hand, which was slowly releasing from Derrick's grip. His hand was covered in blood. It was trickling down from Derrick's headless body. I turned around to the sound of demonic laughter. Every guest gathered around me in a semi circle like a cult. They were beheaded but each guest was holding their severed heads in their own hands. Suddenly, the floor dropped beneath me like a broken elevator. It descended downward. I reached up with my hands to no avail. My mouth was open but no sounds were released. The guests began to throw broken bits of jewelry, phones and appliances. The demon stood in front of the crowd with Portia dressed in gothic black. Her left leg was hoisted and wrapped around his waist. The demon spoke to me and said, "See ya bitch. When they ask how ya got there, tell 'em Scully sent ya!"

Laughter rang out as the floor above me sealed shut.

Sheer terror ripped me from REM sleep. Derrick was waiting to comfort me.

"Hey, hey, you're here, you're ok."

I was shaking uncontrollably, feeling frightened and confused.

"Where, who, oh God." He hugged me for reassurance and said, "You must have been dreaming, you're safe Shanelle."

I relaxed in his arms while he turned on the radio. I looked at the clock; it was 2:00 am. I asked, "How long have I been sleeping?"

He replied, "For three hours. You fell asleep during eyewitness News." Guilt set in.

"Derrick, I'm sooooo sorry, I didn't mean to get like that on...." He didn't let me finish. He kissed my forehead and said, "Baby girl, you deserve to be happy and as long as you are with me, that's what we're gonna do. Let's go downstairs and get some tea."

He slid off the bed and extended his hand to help me up. I perked up and replied in a breathy voice, "Yes Dr. Johnson."

Derrick and I resumed the happy couple role at the kitchen table. He put the pound cake away, neglecting to offer me a piece. I guess the remnants left in the toilet was all he needed to be rude. We played footsie under the table and talked about my next game. Our conversation triggered Portia into consciousness. I pulled my feet away from his and stood up. I needed to change the tone in the room. Leaning against the counter top was a physical anchor at this point. The nausea was gone, but the support of the counter top like the toilet upstairs calmed me down. I looked at him and said, "So, what's up with Portia?"

The question led his eyes to the kitchen floor. Derrick stood up but kept his distance.

"You need to know that this basketball thing is not where my head is at. The only people that do know are Coach Mahoney and my mom."

I quickly interrupted, "Well, I'm listening, but I didn't hear anything about her."

He said, "Well you need to let me finish."

"Ok, ok, I'm sorry, go ahead." The suspense was killing me.

Derrick replied, "I was accepted to Duke University in the early admission's program. Even though it's a sure thing, I took the state regent's exam for an early exit out of St. James Prep. In order to get a jump on things, I'm going to take some advanced biology courses at St. James University. Duke is going to accept those credits as long as I keep an A average."

Derrick had a solid academic background and this news would be of no surprise to anyone that knew him, even Portia. I had to wonder how she fit into this picture. Derrick continued, "Once basketball season is over, I'll be at the university buried in books Shanelle. I slowed him down by putting my fingers over his lips and said, "Is this what you want Derrick?" He stared at me with an assuring smile and said, "It's what I've dreamed about."

With that, I kissed him softly and then released his lips.

"Well, then Dr. Derrick, I am happy for you. Congratulations baby."

Derrick chimed in.

"Not so fast, Sherlock, I haven't answered the million dollar question and I know you're looking for an answer."

"True, true," I replied.

"Well, didn't you notice that she wasn't at the game?"

"Do you think I come to your games to check on her, or you Derrick?" I thought to myself, "Come on now, you're pissing me off." I wasn't checking for that bitch and besides she was going to have a rendezvous with Rashan in a few months.

Derrick chimed in, "Well, I told her two things yesterday and I think she knew it was coming. The first thing was my school plans and the second thing was she and I were over. You know as well as I do that Portia has an insatiable appetite and I can't give her what she needs. She wants the fast lane with a ball player strapped to her hip at her beckon call. I'm not down with that and my news was all she needed to set her free. We had a shallow relationship from the start and I can't believe I stayed with her that long. She made it clear that I should seek you out because she could sense something was going on between us."

"What!" I replied.

"Look Shanelle, I don't care what Portia thinks of you or me, but I do agree with one thing Portia said about you..."

I jumped right in, "What did she say, she doesn't know anything about me!" I was furious.

Derrick moved in closer to me to quiet my hostility.

"Chill Shanelle, chill. Portia has said time and time again that the two of us had a secret love affair without spoken words."

I was so puzzled I had to respond.

"Why would she think to say that?"

He grabbed my hand and said, "How many times have I stopped and stared at you, not knowing what to say or do. I look at you and your eyes speak to me but I can only guess what you're trying to say. I made up the words hoping that one day you would tell me. Don't get me wrong, I want you to tell me what's in your head Shanelle."

Derrick paused in frustration and then took a deep breath.

"Look, Portia said it best yesterday when she said that you and I look at each other in a way that should be captured in a bottle and thrown out to sea and if by chance it washed away on a sunny shore, some pitiful mother fucker would take pleasure in our moment too."

"Damn," I thought, "Portia's trick ass told Derrick off but had it right on the money." I couldn't believe she could be so deep with her shallow ass.

Derrick continued, "She only has herself to blame. She started to go off on you, but I wouldn't let her diss you like that."

He pulled me by the waist into him and said, "Girl, I can't even tell you how many times I have thought about you. It's so bad that I can't even concentrate. I follow you in the papers, come to your games and all we do is stop and stare. When I saw you at the game the other night at the top of the bleachers and you gave me that half of a smile, I knew that I had to get to you somehow, someway. I need to know you Shanelle, I need to get in that head of yours but figure out where I fit in."

Tears began to stream down my face in utter happiness. I cut him off and said, "I feel the same way and I never knew what to say, so I just stopped and stared like some obsessed fan. I kept the fantasies to myself, without telling you because I was only hoping you felt the same way too. Now I'm here and so are you and I can tell you that I am tired of hiding your name in notebooks, sneaking around St. James, taking buses in different directions just to see you and especially doing all of this in Portia's fucking shadow. So if she's gone she better be gone because I won't be able to pick up the pieces of my crazy life if you disappoint me." I started to stutter a bit but gained control again.

"I... I...mean, I'm happy for you and your success, but even with Portia out of the picture, where does that leave me? Am I supposed to give myself to you and then wait until you're set in life? If so, it's too much for me to bare. But I'm standing here right now and I am shaking inside because I can't believe you feel the same way about me."

Derrick grabbed my face with his hands and kissed my tears away. I struggled to get the words out but I kept going.

"If I could capture this moment Derrick and tell you what I'm feeling instead of crying, I would say all of this sounds so corny right now. Just take me upstairs and show me how much I mean to you. We'll figure the rest of this shit out later."

With that, Derrick picked me up and carried me up fourteen carpeted steps. I felt light and incredibly sexy. I tightened my grip around his neck so hard that the garnet ring my father gave me brushed against my cheek. I thought to myself, "Not now daddy, this is too good to be true."

Derrick carried me into his room. It was the first time I really got to see it. The first thing that captivated me was his scent. It was everywhere and it overwhelmed me with pleasure. His room was fashioned in hunter green and navy. There were trophies from his childhood, old hooded sweatshirts and pictures in frames. The pictures were of his grandmother and mother. Derrick laid me down on his bed. The mattress melted into the impression of my frame and I was comforted by the feel of his linens. Derrick stood in between my legs and stared at me like I was a freshly served appetizer. Then he said, "Turn over."

Trusting him completely, I surrendered to his touch. My finger tips touched the head board and he began to move me up so I had enough room to wrap my fingers around the head board with something to hold onto. Derrick got off the bed and turned off the lights. The Whispers came on, and why did it have to be Chocolate Girl? I was through. I drifted off to take in the melodic tune and the feel of a feathery plume being brushed against my inner thighs. He kissed my thighs and I shivered as my nipples began to harden. I felt the mattress sink in as he kneeled on the bed. He began to apply cocoa butter oil to his hands; the smell warmed me in to a rhythmic motion. Derrick began to massage the nape of my neck and my shoulder blades. Tears began to well up in my eyes from his touch. His hands were rough and smooth in different parts as he pressed his fingertips into my skin. He put his lips to my ear and whispered, "I want you, do you want me?"

I was overcome with pleasure and said, "Yes baby."

He whispered in my other ear, "Will you be my lady?" I barely let him finish his sentence, "Yes, baby."

He whispered again to me, "Can I have all of this tonight?"

The answer was too easy, "Of course."

I was lost, crazed and grinding the mattress out. He used both hands to turn me over and gently laid on top of me with all of his clothes on. I tried to release him by pulling down his boxers but he stopped me by locking me down, hand in hand. He slid our hands to the wooden bars and said, "Hold on and bare with me baby, I don't want you to forget tonight."

Surely I would never forget, my dream guy was about to slam me. Vaughn Harper was on WBLS radio station. His smooth voice put me in the right frame of mind. I was relaxed and ready to unwind for Derrick. My breath got heavier and heavier as the Isley Brothers came on. Derrick began to kiss each sensual point on my body. My nipples, stomach and belly button were all at his command and attention. I tried to reach out for him to connect with his strong body but he put my hands back on the headboard.

"Be still baby, or I'm going to tie you up."

I thought to myself, "Oh, I really think I'm going to enjoy that." I laughed out loud at his comment but my laugh brought me back. It was raunchy and mature. My laugh was usually high pitched and petite. It didn't sound right and I began to look around the room to take in the physical reality. I wondered if Portia had been there too, experiencing this with Derrick. I squeezed my eyes to bury thoughts of my Nemesis, I knew she was coming to visit me. Just in time, Derrick kissed me below the belly button and I melted into him by grabbing his head. He quietly whispered, "Shanelle, you smell so good baby."

I thought, "Smell good?" I wasn't wearing any perfume, dear brother stole it and I didn't have the money to buy any. Nemesis began to appear in my confused vision.

"Giving up the Kitty tonight my pretty?" Nemesis asked.

My mind fired back, "Shut up, you'll stop at nothing to see me happy!"

"Happy?" Nemesis asked. "Your father's unhappy right now. Hill Street Blues just went off and that kid smoking pot on the commercial said to your father, 'It's 10:00 pm, do you know your daughter's at Derrick's house trying to get laid?'"

She wasn't through with me either and said, "Oh, your mother just got back from Pathmark. She bought you ten bags of maxi pads. I hope you get your period next month, I don't see him taking a condom out!"

I fired back, but it wasn't in my brain, "Ughhhh, leave me alone!"

Derrick jumped up looking confused and startled.

"Shanelle, what's wrong with you?"

I felt so stupid and betrayed by my conscious.

"No, it's not you." I replied as I grabbed his face for focus. "You're wonderful; it's just that, it's so pleasing to me, but…,"

"What is it, you don't want me to make love to you?" Derrick asked.

Before I could answer, Nemesis fired another shot, "Surely ding-a-ling, this is lust, not love."

I squeezed my eyes to shut her out of my mind and concentrate on Derrick but she was in control.

"No ding..., I mean... dick, no Derrick, I'm sorry, I just get so caught up. I do want you, every pulse in my body is chanting your name, but I just need to feel that this is okay in my head and I just think I'm going crazy when I'm with you sometimes." I kept going and said, "Look, when I wake up in the morning and look at myself in the mirror, I need to be able to smile back at myself. I think we're more than that and I don't want to lose that part of us that is so special."

Derrick rested his hand on my neck as I started to pull my panties up.

"Oh, so after all of that, you just want me to keep flirting with you until I go crazy talking to myself like you were doing?"

I blew the mental trip off because there was a lot more going on. "Derrick you're quite the gentleman. I didn't come here to tease you, but I do have the right to change my mind."

He got off the bed and took a matching sweat suit from out of his closet. There was apparent strain in his face like he had a good case of blue balls.

"Here, put these on, before I forget you're making sense."

Derrick turned on the lights and shut the radio off because there was no more use for the quiet storm. He walked out the room and headed for the shower. I picked up his sweat suit but I didn't put it on. It was bitter cold outside, but his room was roasting warm and I felt comfortable in my nakedness. I got under his covers and rubbed my nipples to dull the sensation of Derrick's touch. Derrick called my name, "Shanelle, can you bring me a towel please?"

I thought to myself, "Well at least he's still speaking to me."

I got a towel for him and went into the bathroom. In all his naked brown glory he was dripping wet with the water running down on him. He started laughing and said, "Girl don't mess with me, I gave you that sweat suit for a reason."

I put the towel on the sink and got in the shower with him.

"Can I join you, oops, I already did, tee, hee."

"Oh, now you want to be a bad girl. Don't start something you can't finish."

"I am a good girl," I replied. "Let me wash your back. Turn around."

He surrendered and turned around. His body was beautiful and lean underneath the swell of the steam. I couldn't resist kissing his smooth brown skin glistening under the running water.

"If you don't wash my back you're gonna be mine in a minute right on the shower floor."

A loud snorting sound escaped from me as I started to laugh and said, "Ok, but at least I can say we took a shower together."

I lathered up the washcloth and washed his beautiful back. With all the strength left in me, I massaged the soap into his skin and rinsed him down. Derrick turned around and kissed me with an open mouth. The warm water caressed the two of us with unbridled pleasure. I could feel his manhood pressed up against me but I was not ready.

Derrick pulled away from me and grabbed the shampoo. He poured some in his hand and began to wash my hair. I felt light headed by his touch. He was so tender and sensitive, despite his need to be inside of me. He turned me around and continued to wash my hair. He slid his lathered hands over my breasts and washed them too. I was in seventh heaven. I turned around and tilted my head back so the water could rinse my hair off while Derrick took one of my breasts in his mouth and the other in his hands.

"I want you so bad girl, but I'm cool."

I looked him in the eyes and softly said, "Yeah, I'm cool too."

As I continued to rinse my hair, Derrick got down on his knees and kissed my legs. I grabbed Derrick's shoulders for support as he took small bites out of my upper thighs and hips. I wanted him to explore other places, but he didn't and that was cool too because I wasn't going to reciprocate. Derrick got off his knees and picked me up. I wrapped my legs around his waist and stared into his eyes. He looked back and said, "I need you to get out so I can take care of big man. Put something on Shanelle if you want to stay with me tonight."

The look on his face meant business. He looked me in the eyes with a serious expression and said, "Is that fair Shanelle?"

"Yes, that's fair," I replied. I slid down and stepped out of the shower. He never took his eyes off of me. I towel dried my hair in front of the mirror. Since I had that twist-a-wave wet look hair I didn't need a blow dryer. Derrick tamed the lion by watching me and released his tension down the drain. I felt bad that he had to do it, but I was glad to give him the visual pleasure he needed to release himself.

"Damn girl, I have dreamt about you and what I would do to you a million times over. The next time you won't be so lucky."

I pretended to hand him the towel but instead I smacked him with it to shock him out of his dazed response.

"Ouch! Oh see, now you've done it!" He jumped out of the shower and ran after me, wet hair, bodies and all. He chased me to the bed and dove on top of me laughing like we laughed during the snowstorm. I felt so comforted by him and my need to feel safe, even though we were completely naked. He tickled me so hard my stomach started to hurt. I couldn't get away, so I begged for mercy.

"Please stop, I'll do anything!"

My laughter reached a high pitch as Derrick replied, "Anything?"

I screamed again, unable to get away. "No, just about anything. Let me go, my stomach hurts!"

He released me and I let out a loud sigh. I stretched out across his bed reaching for my pocketbook. It was a great time to wind him down so I decided to read a poem I wrote for him.

"What's that?" Derrick asked.

"Oh, just a little poem I wrote to keep me sane, do you want to hear it?"

"Sure, and it better be good."

"Ok," I said. "This piece is titled, 'This or That' by Shanelle Brown."

Derrick crossed his arms as I cleared my throat in jest.

"Is it this that you want, the cream in my mind, our eyes making love without the physical grind. My flow cries out sweet passion for you, but don't touch my waist, don't touch my boobs. I grimace with intensity the pleasures I fear. My cat eyes of passion draw you near. Indeed it will be the best you've had, but stop, don't touch, I promised my dad!"

Derrick cracked up, "Oh, he's responsible for my blue balls?"

"Shut up and let me finish." I cleared my throat again to get his undivided attention.

"At the age of thirteen daddy gave me to hold, three carats garnet, wrapped in white gold. He slid it on my ring finger to have and to hold. Lead with your mind, it's stronger and bold. Your heart will mislead you, this I fear, and I'll take that punk out like a hunter to a deer." I held up my left hand and proudly displayed my shield of virtue and protection. *"Wear your shield of virtue and stay three steps ahead, a romp and roll means nothing to a boy in bed. So if it's "this" that you want, you can't have it, it's mine, we'll meet in ten years for a meeting of the mind."*

I stood up and took my bow as he clapped for me.

"You don't think I'm a boy Shanelle?"

"No, but my daddy does." I looked at him so he could understand my intentions.

"Hey, my poem needs some work, but it's a general thing, don't take it personal."

Derrick rubbed the side of my leg and said, "I'm not, baby girl. Anyway, I have something for you."

My eyes lit up with excitement and I was tickled with delight. "For me, lil' ole' me?"

Derrick got up and went to the closet. I sat up with curiosity as he pulled out a brown hatbox and sat on the bed next to me. He put his hands on the box and said, "Shanelle, I hope you don't think I'm crazy as you are, but I've been meaning to give you these things that mean a lot to me. While I'm gone, I want you to get through this thing that's going on but if it gets too rough, I'm here for you. It's one of the reasons that I stopped when you asked me to because I don't want to make you feel vulnerable if we don't work out. I look at you and I admire your courage and tenacity and yet I feel like I can't help you get through this because you're not very open about the whole thing."

My eyes started to swell up. I wanted to tell him everything, but it was too much to put on him and certainly not his problem. Derrick continued, "I wish I didn't have to leave you behind, but I am. I won't be able to pick you up or keep you safe when you need me. So I put some things in a box for you to remember that I am with you and to be strong until things get better."

He took the top of the box off and a green felt leg popped out. He opened the box and out came Kermit the Frog. With little girl glee I replied, "Kermie!"

I gave him a big hug as Derrick laughed at my girlish behavior. Like a child on Christmas morning, I exclaimed, "What else have you got for me?" Derrick smiled and said, "Close your eyes pretty lady."

I closed my eyes, but when he said things like that I wanted to jump on him again and break my own rules of engagement. I politely said, "Ready when you are." With that I felt something familiar rest on me. It smelled and felt familiar to me as he laid it across my shoulders.

I opened my eyes and confirmed that it was his varsity jacket, a coveted trophy for any girl in my town. I put the jacket on and tucked the rest of the jacket into my body. The feel of his fabric on me was heavenly and comforting. I jumped up on the bed and began to cheer for him, "Derrick, Derrick, he's my man, if he can't do it no one can!"

He couldn't resist a comeback and said, "So you're going to let me do it?"

I chimed in on top of his sentence, "No, silly, but I'll be willing to wait for you."

My comment seemed to sadden him so I stopped jumping up and down to pay closer attention.

"What is it?" Derrick grabbed my hand and said, "Shanelle, a lot is going to happen to the two of us over the next year and I'm hoping things will get better. But if I know you the way I think I do, it won't be long before you find a guy who will be perfect for you and give you the things you need. I'm just in the wrong place right now, but I would love to be that guy."

His words seemed so silly. I could not conceive liking anyone as much as Derrick.

"Don't be silly, you're all I need."

Derrick didn't respond this time, I guess he just took it all in and tried to make sense of it for himself.

"Ok Shanelle, I won't think about it anymore, but I would love it if you were still here waiting for me when I come home."

I gave him a hug and said, "Baby, we've just begun, I'll be here."

Little did I know then that it would never happen in our lifetime.

Eyewitness News came on the TV. Storm Fields announced that unseasonably warm weather from the Midwest would be mixed with bright sun causing temperatures to reach sixty-five degrees. Derrick sat up and said, "Wow, sixty-five degrees for December, we need to take advantage of that."

I sat up next to him curious about his plans. "What do you want to do?"

"Let's drive down to the beach," Derrick said.

"The beach," I replied, "Derrick, it's freezing!" The idea sounded absurd to me. I had very little exposure to the New Jersey shore up until now, but I was open to the idea as long as I was with him.

"Well we're not going swimming silly, but the ocean view will get your mind off of things."

I snuggled into his neck and said, "Well I can't wait, as long as I am with you, I'm cool."

"Yeah, we're cool, huh?"

I laughed and closed my eyes with the security of Derrick holding me. It was picture perfect. He in his sweat pants and sweatshirt and me in my varsity jacket, no bra and pink satin panties.

Vision of Him

By morning we were heading down Parkway South to exit 98, Belmar, New Jersey. With just four hours of sleep, I was alert, chatty and craving a hot chocolate. I made sure to pay attention to every directional detail. There would come a day when I had my license and I was going to come back with the girls. I memorized the railroad, the WaWa and the turn onto Sixteenth Avenue. By 9 am, there were people out and about walking and jogging on the boardwalk. We walked onto the beach with our shoes on. I was wearing a navy Nike track suit with sneakers to match. The pants were a new cotton spandex blend that absorbed sweat and gave my legs incredible form. Besides, I wanted to be comfortable just in case we decided to break out in a heat of passion. Derrick looked good as usual in his trademark sweats with a black turtleneck underneath. We looked good together as he led me to a spot on the sand about fifty feet from the shore line. He opened his sand chair which was big enough for the two of us, although I chose to sit in between his legs. Off in the distance, a group of guys caught my attention as Derrick wrapped his arms around me. The sun was very bright so I used my hand as a visor to see them. They were playing touch football, appearing as silhouettes in the distance. One of them seemed to stand out among the rest. Derrick nuzzled his face in my neck and snuggled into me for warmth. The position on the sand gave me a better angle of the game. As I watched them play, Derrick sang love songs to me and nibbled on my ear. It complemented the moment, but as he continued, the silhouette football game came visibly closer to us. I took a deep breath as the mighty one came closer. His face turned in my direction as he positioned his pass like the poster boy for the Heisman trophy. Like a match connected to a Fourth of July sparkler, I sat up to embrace his physiology and dark chocolate vision. He was cinnamon brown, with glistening skin under the sunlight. He was slightly over six feet tall with a firm husky neck and broad shoulders. I found myself floating away from Derrick's love song to look more intently at this warrior. The game drew closer to us, at least three feet and I began to feel loose particles of sand as they ran by. He turned to receive a pass and his burgundy sweatshirt said a little bit about him. I thought to myself, "Hmmm, Lakewood Athletics."

One thing was true, he was a man and not a boy. His body was absolutely beautiful. He had a cut waist and powerful thighs. Derrick began to stroke my hair and I smiled as the warrior looked my way. The warrior smiled back even though my smile was a reaction to Derrick's innocent affection for me. Suddenly the warrior motioned to Derrick with the football as he walked up to our blanket. In a deep burley voice he said, "Yo man, you want in, we need another player?"

The base in Derrick's voice seemed to triple in his response, "Nah man, I'm cool in my spot."

To my surprise, the brazen Dark Gable towering over us peered down at me and said, "How about you little lady?"

My mouth dropped open but nothing came out. Derrick answered the question before I could form a thought.

"Nah man, she's cool too."

The guys in the game laughed out loud and said, "Leave 'em along Q-Dog and get back in the game."

Derrick squeezed me tight and said, "Even the college boys want you, but you're all mine."

I wondered how Derrick knew they were in college, but I didn't ask. I was curious about Mr. Cinnamon and what his deal was. He was arrogant, self assured and down right brazen for walking up on us, but I was incredibly excited to get his attention. More importantly, I wanted to know his name. Kitty nestled around and snuggled in for a nap, but I wanted the warrior to push Derrick down and carry me off into the sunset. The thought of what the warrior would do to me was thought provoking and it made me put my pointer finger in my mouth and smile devilishly. Derrick asked me to get up because he needed to go to the bathroom. I in turn wanted a hot chocolate to soothe me while I watched the rest of the game. Derrick asked if I needed anything and I told him I was going to go across the street for something hot. He gave me twenty dollars and asked for bottled water. He headed down the boardwalk and I crossed the street at Sixteenth Avenue to go to Dunkin 'Donuts. I went inside and smelled the aroma of fresh coffee and donuts. My mouth started to water as I mentally resisted the thought of eating three chocolate-frosted donuts. Just then, I felt a presence behind me. I continued to move up in the line but every time I inched forward, the person behind kept invading my space. Then a male voice spoke to me.

"So, is pretty boy your boyfriend?"

I turned to face my aggressor and to my surprise it was the mighty one, perhaps he was ready to take me away but I wasn't nervous. I reacted abruptly as I faced the warrior who was just smiling at me on the beach.

"No, he's just a friend, why do you ask?" I paused and said, "Oh would you excuse me please."

I turned to face the cashier, put a dollar on the table and said, "One large hot chocolate, sweet please." I turned to face him and said, "Why do you ask?"

His smile was as confident as Billy Dee Williams.

"Well, he's not your type that's for sure."

My eyes got really wide and I thought to myself, "No he didn't just say that!"

He advanced the tease by mimicking my expression with a cocky ass grin on his face. I fired back with pride and sensuality and said, "Oh, like you know my type?"

He cocked his head to the side and said with another grin, "He can't handle you, you've got that look in your eye and I know you wanted to get up and play some contact football, maybe even one on one."

He laughed on the inside and said, "Anyway, you're young and I don't want to mess up your puppy love, but here's a tip, if you want to get rid of those dark circles under your eyes, give up hot chocolate, get more rest and drink pure water."

My face got all fired up. "Excuse me, I didn't need all of that and besides you're in this Dunkin' Donuts with me." I grabbed my hot chocolate and put the change in the tip jar.

The warrior was ready for me and said, "Yeah, but I'm just buying the Sunday paper. If I knew you better, I would offer to take you to church with me to get some of that worry out of your head, you're too serious little girl."

I wanted to smack him after that comment, he was breaking me down layer by layer and he sounded like a religious fanatic to boot. I turned to walk out and I could see Derrick heading to the store to rescue me. I didn't need rescuing though, I was a fighter and I wanted to tell this guy off. He asked, "You're not from around here are you?"

I clutched my dark eye inducing drink and gripped it firmly. I didn't answer at first so he responded as Derrick crossed the street.

"Go have a talk with God, get organized and you'll make a way on your own terms. When you're finished kicking it with pretty boy in a couple of years, take the Parkway back to exit 98 and bring those big pretty legs with you."

My mouth hung open in pure disbelief at his commentary. As he walked out, Derrick walked in. The cashier shouted to him, "See you next week Alex."

Through the glass pane Alex waved a peace sign to the cashier and then he winked at me. Derrick went to the concession area and asked for water. I couldn't believe I was distracted so bad that I forgot to get Derrick's water. He put his arm around my shoulder and said, "I can't leave you alone for a minute."

Suddenly my equilibrium seemed off and I was ready to leave. Everything "Alex" said to me was the truth and it was all for me to figure out. I took a sip of my hot chocolate and then threw it in the garbage can at the corner of Sixteenth Avenue. Derrick looked surprised and said, "Hey, I thought you wanted that?"

I looked to see where the warrior went. He climbed into a Mazda RX 7 and sped off. Suddenly there was a change in me.

"No, it wasn't that good, I want to go home, I'm getting cold."

Derrick didn't ask what was wrong. He met my every need, no matter what I said. We went back to our spot and folded the blankets. I looked at Derrick and wondered what would happen to the two of us once we got back home. I only had one pet peeve so I said to him, "Derrick can you promise me one thing?"

"What is it?" Derrick replied.

"If I run into you and you're with your boys, will you promise not to act shady?"

"What makes you think I would do something like that?" Derrick asked. He seemed puzzled by the question.

"You know how you guys are, pretending to be something different around your friends and when it's just us, you act yourself."

Derrick folded the blanket and rested it on his chest and said, "Shanelle, the only thing I did different around you was keep it inside, that's not me. Besides, there's a lot to be said about me taking a cold shower tonight for you girl. But you'll see I am not the average guy."

Derrick put his arms around me and gave me a reassuring hug. I nestled my chin into his shoulders taking in the panoramic view of the ocean. I held on to his hug as he rocked me back and forth. The ocean looked so majestic, yet mysterious and inviting. I was comforted by Derrick's touch but the invitation Alex extended was certainly one that I had to follow up on. Derrick packed up the car while I sat inside looking out the window.

On the way home I played the scene out in my mind as Derrick held my free hand. Derrick the rescuer and provider, always there for me, but along comes a mysterious stranger who blows my mind with a few simple sentences. Sure, I know how to pack a duffel bag, but what about my life? Where was I going and why was I in constant flight? He was right and he barely knew me. I needed to do those things and I definitely wanted to see him again. I took out my journal and wrote a poem to remember him. I held the front cover of my journal up so Derrick couldn't peak. I didn't want to disappoint him. I looked into my compact and smiled at myself before I began to write. The circles around my eyes were dark, but sleep and water could cure those issues. Crossing over the bridge on that unseasonably warm day in December, I should have thanked Derrick a million times or more. Our journey to the beach was my prelude to someone new. Little did I know it wouldn't be long before we would meet again. About him, I wrote:

Drawn to him,
his skin
so cinnamon.
Will you let me in,
to your mind,
unwind,
my thoughts of you
like the suckle of sweet honeydew.
I need to get to know you.
I need to know your name,
sitting with this current boy,
visions of you
driving me insane.
Oh that's your name
your boy just exclaimed,
"Yo Alex, I got next."
But I want a turn.
Your cinnamon vision,
fires and burns
a critical synapse
in my brain
look at me
make me sane
but take your time,
I'm just a girl.
You are certainly a man.
This sunny day I understand,
That contained in your vision,

A master plan
unearth my girlish gem to woman from man.
I need to be me,
this precious star drawn to you
wherever you are.

I smiled when I closed my journal shut. It was a clever piece and poetry seemed to calm me in my crazy reality. I began to focus on Derrick again as we talked about his future plans and how he was going to break the news to all his boys. I was genuinely happy for Derrick, but I knew that his absence would overwhelm me just the same.

We parked in North Orange Park and talked some more before he took me home. I wanted it to last forever but it was overshadowed by a familiar face walking by. I tried to pretend not to notice but dear brother had a way of making you pay attention. He walked right up to Derrick's window and made his presence known by knocking on the driver's window.

"Yo, what up nigga?"

Derrick barely flinched as he rolled down the window.

"Do I know you man?"

Steven started laughing, "Yo, I don't give a fuck if you know me or not, but you know my sister now don't ya?"

I gave Derrick the look like, "Yeah, that's crazy ass, can't you tell?"

Derrick got out of the car and I immediately jumped out and ran around to their side. Derrick was smooth in his approach and he didn't seem scared. He was taller than Steven and it looked like he weighed more, but I was sure Derrick never carried a weapon. A police cruiser just so happened to drive by on South Center Street. Thank goodness the car passed by slowly because it broke dear brother's concentration. Steven walked away laughing, "You better be glad they're out here or I would bust a cap in your ass, nigga"

Derrick laughed back while I admired his confidence. Dear brother on the other hand was not amused and said, "Yeah, pretty boy, next time yo' ass better be ready bitch."

Derrick shrugged him off by waving his hand at him. Steven pointed at me and said, "I'll make sure mom knows her slutty daughter was with one of the Debarge brothers."

I tried not to pay attention to him, but I knew he was going to get me for that mishap. I could only imagine what he would try to do. I pleaded with Derrick to drive me home as fast as he could drive.

We jumped in the car and sped past Steven and got to the house first. Even though dear brother was fucked up, we still went through sibling rivalry with Mrs. Viv and I wasn't taking any chances in him convincing her that I wasn't at Candy's house. Derrick pulled in the front of the house and I gave him a quick kiss.

"I'll call you later, don't worry, I'll be fine."

My luck had run out as soon as Steven turned the corner and greeted us with an evil look on his face. He gave Derrick the middle finger and walked to the front door. I grabbed my bags and ran to the door feeling desperate and five minutes short of a good whipping.

Breathing in heavily, I begged for dear brother's mercy.

"Please don't tell mommy, okay Steven, please? I started desperately rummaging through my pocketbook hoping to find at least ten dollars to pay his ass off until I got paid. He surveyed every inch of my bag looking for the same thing and said, "This one's gonna cost you, I want whatever you have now, plus fifty when you get paid next week."

I looked him in the eye nodding my head in approval. "Ok, ok, but please don't tell mommy."

My heart was racing so fast, I thought it was going to jump out of my body. Mrs. Viv opened the door and started raging, "Get your ass in here Shanelle and clean that damn refrigerator out like I told you and next week you better have your ass in church instead of hanging in the streets."

I gave Mrs. Viv a kiss and said, "Ok momma, do you want me to clean the mirrors too?"

"Do you need to ask Shanelle? Don't get cute with me, Kena is coming tonight and I want this place clean, do you hear me?"

I quickly replied, "Ok, no problem." Steven looked at the two of us with disgust in his eyes. I was sure he wanted to kill me in front of Mrs. Viv but he needed that fifty bucks on Friday and that would certainly stall his sibling homicide plot. He retreated to the attic without a word. Mrs. Viv had no work assignments for Steven. I suppose she did not want to overload his brain with too much talk and activity. She yelled upstairs and said to him, "Steven, I'll call you when dinner's ready."

His response was the slam of the attic door and her response was putting on WNJR for the last hour of gospel tunes. With that little episode working well in my favor, I cleaned the refrigerator out and wiped down the glass mirrors. I was in a great mood and the smells emitting from the kitchen enhanced my good feeling and thoughts of Derrick. I was humming so loud, Mrs. Viv could not resist a motherly inquiry, "You're in a good mood missy, what's new with you?"

I responded quickly, "Nothing!"

She leaned back reacting to my response.

"Whoa, I was just asking a simple question Shanelle."

"Oh, I'm sorry mom, I've been preoccupied with the season and all the games coming up."

That seemed to trigger something in Mrs. Viv because her face changed to a serious expression.

"I've been meaning to talk to you about the season Shanelle."

She didn't finish her sentence to my satisfaction so I had to ask. "What about the season?"

"Well, your father and I have been struggling with all these medical bills and we're going to need you to get a job when your birthday comes around to cover your personal expenses."

"What!?" My tone was high pitched and hostile causing Mrs. Viv to stand up and pay attention.

"Lower your tone of voice. You heard me girl. You're going to have to get a job after school to cover your expenses because your father and I are barely making ends meet."

I was irate and frustrated. I looked at her and shouted, "Why can't Steven get a job? He sits around here all day listening to Richard Pryor, getting high and stealing from us all the time, that's not fair!"

Little did I know, Steven was at the top of the stairs taking in my plot. He bolted down the stairs and lit into my ass.

"Yeah mom, Shanelle has plenty of time to work, she was with Derrick all weekend and if she's got time to do the do, she can get a job until I get better."

Not only did I rat him out, he took my money and ratted me out. I couldn't make sense of anything because before I knew it, a backhand was crashing against my face sending me to the floor. Mrs. Viv was good for smacking first and then asking questions later.

"Is that true Shanelle?" I tried to recover, but the two of them were too much for me to conjure up a lie. Besides, the vicious cycle of lies, payoffs and thievery was ridiculous. I yelled back at Mrs. Viv to her surprise.

"Fine! I'll quit playing so he can keep on smokin' weed, maybe I'll turn over all of my paychecks to his fucked up ass until he finally kills me!"

I jumped up and bolted upstairs to my room. They were right behind me but I was too quick for them. The drama was too much for dear daddy so he got up and came to my bedroom door. I made sure to lock the door with the skeleton key so they couldn't get in and gang up on me.

"Shanelle, open this door now!" Nobody's going to lock doors in my house damnit."

I laid face down on the bed and started to cry. Is she serious? Everyone's locking their door, job or not, just to prevent dear brother from stealing from us. It seemed like I was shrinking in my bed. I wanted to disappear in the sheets but it didn't happen.

The three musketeers stood outside my door begging and pleading for me to come out to plot their revenge, but the time wasn't right, a horn blew out front, one that was familiar to all of us. It was Mrs. Viv's first cousin Marvin. Luckily, his arrival took the attention off of me but set my mother off in a different direction. They stood outside the hallway arguing over our cousin. Dear dad started first, "Vivian, you didn't tell me Marvin was coming."

Mrs. Viv responded nervously, "I didn't know he was coming either, he never called, damn! I know he's going to clog our toilet again."

I peaked out the window to get a look at the freak of nature. Marvin was five foot five inches tall and weighed at least five hundred and forty pounds. I was amazed that he could still get around with his oxygen mask. Marvin loved to come unannounced on Sundays to eat up Mrs. Viv's southern fried chicken. The vegetable oil Mrs. Viv used always did a number on his rotten belly because he would hit the bathroom the minute he finished with the vilest odor on the planet. I likened it to a rotten corpse, sour milk and three-day old broccoli. He spent most of his time talking about the King James Version of the bible and interpreting the verses in a way that justified his gluttony. His behavior and mounting weight gain sickened my father, but in an odd way, he enjoyed Marvin's company. Since no one cleaned the bathroom except me, I was the one who had to don hazmat clothes to clean up after his waste and stench.

I released the blinds as he reached the top of the stoop. Tears started to trickle down my face. I needed a way out. Maybe I could just run away and Candy's parents could adopt me. Surely Candy doesn't have this kind of drama going on. She didn't even have a brother. I couldn't live with Bonnie, because her mother wouldn't allow it and would probably take sides with my mother since they've known each other for ten years. The tears kept flowing but the release felt good. I could hear Marvin in the background downstairs complaining about his arthritis and all of his other ailments. I was waiting for an opportune time to go downstairs and walk straight out the door. But I was just too tired and needed to sleep. Then the thought of giving up basketball. How could I tell the coach? But if they were going to cut me off because of dear brother's medical bills, there was nothing left to do but quit and get a job. I needed to get to the city on the weekends, buy makeup and sanitary products. I yelled into the pillow, "God I hate this shit, if I can just find a way out of here I swear I'll never come back!"

Mrs. Viv yelled from downstairs, "Shanelle, come downstairs and say hi to your cousin." I wiped my tears away, cleared my throat and yelled back, "Ok, in a minute!" I wiped my face with my blanket and went downstairs. The happy family was assembled in the living room talking about Reaganomics. They could all tell that I was crying but Marvin was the curious outsider who asked first, "Everything ok Shanelle?" Dear brother could not tolerate my response and got up and left the room. I tried to respond but couldn't remember if I locked my door. Funny, Steven didn't go upstairs. As I stood there talking to Marvin, he was busy raiding Marvin's jacket for money. I wanted to yell, "Thief, thief!" But it would have served no useful purpose for me. Steven was good at lying and talking his way out of the worst situations. Things needed to go my way for a while. I needed to ease the tension between me and Mrs. Viv so I could work my way back to Derrick. Dinner was served without a hitch and as I expected, I had to go upstairs and clean up after Marvin. It was vile as I had expected, but the welcomed break from the domestic monotony downstairs was a relief. As I cleaned the bathroom, I tried to organize a checklist of things that were due in school the next day. Surely I was going to flunk my Spanish exam. I didn't look at the chapter book in three weeks and I was really behind. With the season mid way through, I was in jeopardy of being kicked off anyway. Maybe a job could keep me out of the house each day until everyone got home and then dear brother could stay off my back. I flushed the toilet one last time until all the debris disappeared. Over and over my inner voice spoke to me about getting organized. The mysterious stranger was so right. I wanted to see him again to ask him how he knew so much about me, but for now, my only resolve was to figure it out myself.

Devil's Dormancy

The next day the temperature dropped twenty degrees. Derrick dropped me off to a seemingly tranquil house. Quiet and defeated, I walked into the house. Derrick made his announcement, I flunked my Spanish exam and I didn't want to talk to Derrick about not seeing him for two weeks because of his hectic academic schedule. To make matters worse, Aunt Flo was due to arrive and as each day crept up on me, all I could do was sleep. I walked in the house and took in the silence. Kiko came from the kitchen wagging his tail, which was a good sign and usually meant that dear brother was out and about. I motioned Kiko to go upstairs so he could scout out any unusual activity. If dear brother was trying to scare me, Kiko would surely give him away. Luckily it was just me in the house, so I jumped in the shower and washed my hair. Kiko was waiting faithfully outside the door, which was another sign that the house was empty. When times got rough, Kiko ran away too and then return with a few bumps and bruises. He always managed to find his way home if that's supposed to mean something. I climbed across my bed and took in the pleasure of tranquility. Kiko's ears popped up and he headed downstairs, I could hear dear brother in the distance petting the dog and encouraging him to go to the basement. I sat up on my bed alert and ready. Mom and dad were not home yet but dear brother was pretty tranquil on Monday nights. He came up the stairs and walked right in my room.

"What's up Nell?" I was cold and to the point.

"Nothing."

"That's all you've got to say to me with the weekend you had. How was school today?"

He was pissing me off with his sheer arrogance like he really cared how I was doing.

"What's your point, you don't care if I live or die?"

He got indignant this time, "You better watch your mouth fatty patty before I knock you out!"

"Yeah okay, Steven!"

"Yeah, whatever nothin', you better watch your back bitch."

Before he left he sucked his teeth long and hard and then motioned his hands like he was stabbing someone. He went up to his room and put on a Richard Pryor album. As soon as Richard opened his mouth, Steven started laughing. I couldn't stand when he played it because I knew that he was smoking weed for better effects. I turned on the TV to tune him out. The bottom of the TV flashed a weather report calling for a winter storm watch scheduled for midnight into tomorrow afternoon. My heart sank again. In my house that was a death sentence because dear brother would surely fire up his evil wrath. The thought of it brought him into satirical laughter like he heard my thoughts. The high was taking effect and if you smelled hard enough, you could catch a wiff. He called me from upstairs, he was always looking for an audience.

"Yo Nell, Rich is funnier than a mother fucker, Ha, haaaa!"

I just shook my head in sheer hatred. The most I'm doing is trying to go to school and do the right thing and he's upstairs in the get high attic with quarterly stays in rehabilitation hospital. Before I knew it, I drifted off to sleep. In an hour, I jumped up realizing that I didn't lock my door for the night. I looked out the window and noticed the car was back. I got up, went to the bathroom and peered into my parents' room. They were both sound asleep, worn out from church service. I locked myself in my room. There was a note from Mrs. Viv with a face drawn on it. She wrote, "Shanelle, you're grounded. I had no idea where you were and you were not at Candy's house. Take your ass to school tomorrow and come straight home."

Where the note ended, the demon drew his infamous angry face and wrote the following satirical message:

"I told you your ass was grass you fat Mother Fucker."

I tore the note up and threw it on the floor. How the hell am I going to get organized when my ass is stuck here with nowhere to go? I looked around the room and noticed my closet was open. My new Nike sneakers were missing and less than two months old. I wanted to cry but rapid breathing kicked in and my head started spinning forcing me to sit down. I put my head between my legs and took long deep breaths. I learned that technique from my basketball coach. It helped me whenever I got really nervous before a game. It had little effect on me tonight, because I was tired of the stupid house rules under the cloak of sheer mental terror. I double checked my door and then climbed in bed. My sheets and comforter were heavy and warm. I took refuge by covering my head and quickly went back to sleep. By the time I woke up it was already 8:30 am. The TV was still on and it was clear that the snowstorm shut the schools and government offices down. I knew Mrs. Viv had to work because with the public schools closed she would have to be on duty to supervise the community center. On days like this, she usually took me to work to volunteer with the preschool children. I imagined that she was so angry at me that she wouldn't be able to stomach the sight of my face let alone accompany her to work. As for dad, he never missed a day of work and was annually awarded for his attendance. I think they were both glad to wake up and go to a job. I was quickly interrupted into reality as the beast started his reign of terror. He started pounding on my door and shouted, "Get up bitch and take a shower before I cut the fucking water off!"

I shouted back at him through the door, "Go take your fucking medicine and leave me the hell alone!"

He used one finger to bang on the door this time. He was furious and hell bent on proving it to me.

"I only need cold water bitch, you better hurry too, the pipes are going to freeze any minute."

I shook my head in disbelief, discouraged that we were going to have another obsessed winter.

"Steven, daddy never shuts the water off, don't get crazy on me again with that pipe shit."

His voice rested in a deeper tone.

"Well I'm turning them off, so leave bitch and take your fucking bags with you."

He wasn't finished because his finger was still banging on the door.

"I'll be sure to lock the door behind you and while you're at it, bang on the window for a fucking mayonnaise sandwich so you can see how that shit feels."

I blurted out a stupid and regrettable answer, "I'm telling daddy on you!"

He loved it and teased me incessantly for my childish responses.

"Daaaadeee, daaadee, I'm telling, boo, hoo, whah, whah. You need a pacifier to go with that fucking phone call."

He used his forehead to beat on the door.

"You dumb bitch, you've got to come out of that room to use the phone fat ass."

I began to feel my menstrual cramps. The two combined sent me over the edge and I was desperate. I shouted through the door and kicked it back, "Leave me alone! I got my fucking period Steven!"

Silence followed. I think he was disgusted by the response and I personalized him by calling him by his name. Sometimes he cut me some slack. He knew that I had terrible cramps as young as ten years old and his empathy diminished his psychotic behavior at least once a month.

He went into the attic and started his symphony of terror. He played Super Freak, Voices, and Super Nature over and over again. He stomped his feet to deepen the effect. I covered my ears and put my hands over my belly. The sound of his music blasting and my cramps was driving me insane. He turned the music down and forgot about his empathy. Steven shouted from the top of the attic stairs, "Three more inches and I'm fucking shit up. I'm starting with you first Shanelle, you bitch and I'm going to gut you like a fish."

I immediately grabbed my bag, threw on some sweats and opened the door quietly with my key. He heard me and started up again.

"This is my house, so get the fuck out."

I walked down the stairs with one coat on my sleeve and headed into the winter snowstorm. I looked back at the house for my own safety. He was standing in Mrs. Viv's window mimicking a knife with his pointer finger across his throat. At that point I decided that I was never going back. Someone would surely hear my story and adopt me. I wasn't a bad kid either. I knew how to cook, clean, baby sit and do whatever was necessary to get a good night sleep. The snow was piercing into my face cracking it with each crystallized snowflake. There was no beauty around me either. I vowed to hate every winter for the rest of my life. I pushed through the deep heavy snow without consideration of nature's fury. There was one back at the house that made up for every weather pattern. There was no hope back there and no need to go back. If my parents sent the police after me, I was going to tell them that they beat me. A good foster home was a better shot than living with Steven. I looked up to the heavens and squinted my eyes at the mystery above.

"Do You hear me God, I'm talking to You, did I just leave the devil behind because I can't take it anymore."

The faster I walked, the heavier my cramps became. My flow was on so hard and steady I was sure if I sat down I would have an accident on my clothes. I needed to get to Bonnie's house quick and I prayed that she was home because I needed to take a shower. Tears started streaming down my face as I dialed her number. Faithfully, Bonnie picked up the phone. By this point I was crying uncontrollably.

"Shanelle, what's wrong, where are you?"

She knew me long enough to know that my muffled sentence

was a stress signal. She remained calm and said, "Stay at the Exxon station, me and Poppy will be there in a few minutes, don't cry."

I could not hold back my tears. I was too frustrated to do anything less. I was tired and I couldn't take the torture. My cramping stopped, so I took the time to search my bag for a dime to call Mrs. Viv. She answered, but she was not happy when she heard the tone in my voice.

"What's that dear, you and Steven are not getting along, ok sweetie, I'll pick you up at Bonnie's after work."

She probably wore that mask because her boss was around. Lord knows she took off so much in the past that her job was in constant jeopardy. I spotted Bonnie's father coming down the hill. Poppy looked angry and worried for me. He knew our family well and could not believe that my brother turned out to be a sour apple. I jumped in Bonnie's car and laid across the back seat to comfort my cramps. Bonnie had bad cramps too and assured me she had some Pamprin back at the house. I went upstairs in Bonnie's room and pulled out some fresh clothes to put on. She knew me long enough to not ask a lot of questions because it only upset me. I took a long shower, which helped me calm down. Bonnie came to the door and said that school was closed tomorrow due to the storm.

"Your mom also called and said to stay overnight at our house. Are you hungry?" Bonnie asked.

"No, I need some sleep if you don't mind."

"Ok chica, I'll be downstairs if you need me."

At last I finally got some rest. I think I slept for twelve hours. I was awakened by someone rubbing my shoulder blade. It was Mrs. Viv and she looked visibly shaken. I was so disoriented it took me a while to figure out that I was still in Bonnie's room. Mrs. Viv rubbed my arm again to lightly wake me from my sleep. I opened my eyes again and stared at her. Her eyes were blood shot red and swollen like she had been crying for hours. She smiled at first but then tears welled up in her eyes and turned her smile into a frown. She simply said, "Steven is in a psychiatric institution, he can't hurt you anymore."

I sat up in disbelief and asked, "Where?"

Mrs. Viv took her time as she spoke. "The police took him to East Orange General Hospital for a twenty-four hour psychiatric evaluation. He was in bad shape Shanelle. It was enough to commit him to Marlboro down in South Jersey. He won't be coming home anytime soon."

She looked around Bonnie's room and smiled. "She has such a cute room, we should get your room painted and fixed up just like

Bonnie's."

That went right over my head. That suggestion would no doubt come with a heavy price. I picked up my duffel bag and started putting my things inside. Mrs. Viv stood up and said, "I'll meet you downstairs, your father's waiting in the car." Her words didn't provide immediate comfort. I knew Mrs. Viv felt terrible for having to commit dear brother, but daddy must have had enough of his behavior. All the money they spent on him was reduced to a commitment. Lock him up and throw away the key was how I looked at the situation. As I walked to the top of the stairs, Bonnie was there to hug me.

"Shanelle, hopefully you'll feel safe now." I didn't say anything; there was nothing to be said because I went through it before. The thoughts of running away left me, but I still needed to get organized.

The ride home was deafening to me as Dad slowly drove down Crescent Avenue pulling on his cigarette. I guess he meant what he said and the choice came at a hard price. We were a family of three plus the dog. Hopefully, dear brother's revolt would seem like a shallow memory even though the wounds were deep. I walked into the hallway and there were images left behind that the struggle to get Steven out of the house was not easy. There were scratch marks in the walls and thick black markings on the hardwood floors. There were wet footprints everywhere and three cracked mirrors that distorted the image of myself in the living room mirrors. From the look of things, even though he was gone, it looked like Steven won. Mrs. Viv took comfort in daddy's arms and wept. If she witnessed the struggle with the police, it must have killed her to sign the commitment papers. I looked down at the floor again and saw bloodstains. I found out the next day that Kiko, in his devotion to Mrs. Viv, protected her honor by lunging in front of Steven and took a mortal stab wound to his lungs. The police had arrived just in time to stop his deadly attack. Even if Mrs. Viv wanted to forgive her son, the police and the prosecutor's office would not let his acts go unpunished. With enough probable cause, they entered the attic and removed three duffel bags of domestic weaponry, including a bat with nails sticking out of the head. I shutter to think what could have happened to me if I stayed that night. Surely I would have been his first target and certainly not his last. The police were kind enough to dispatch an emergency rescue vehicle from animal control to discreetly take Kiko's lifeless body from the house. I couldn't look at the scenery anymore so I went up to my room and unlocked the door. No sigh of relief came with the view of my room. I was convinced he was coming back and I would have to start sleeping with one eye open again. I took another shower and climbed in the bed. Whenever Aunt Flo was in town it seemed like I couldn't get enough sleep.

I rested my head on the pillow for a while and thought about all the things that I lost. The material things were a constant reminder but the childhood memories were harder to deal with. I thought to myself, "He was a great brother when I was little. He taught me how to ride a bike, roller skate and throw a knuckle ball. He let me win King of the Mountain and pushed me down countless hills on my skateboard. For all accounts, he was my hero. But why did he have to do this to himself?"

Tears startled to trickle down my face and on my pillow. I couldn't help but think, "Is his mind that crazy? Am I crazy too?" Lord knows the voices in my head made up for a twenty-piece marching band.

Thinking about it became too much to bear, so I closed my eyes tight hoping everything would go away.

Something Old Something New

The holidays rolled in and out without incident. Spring came early that year. I was happy to see new life in yellow tulips and daffodils. Even though the spring tulips came in beautifully that year, signs of new life were anything short of death in my house. Mrs. Viv, suffering from bouts of limbo loss, mourned and celebrated dear brother at a whim. She was happy one moment, and sadistically sad the next. The house was never clean enough for her and she was constantly making an extra plate of food for him. Me and dad refused to question her habits, not knowing whether it would deepen her into more silence. We probably all needed counseling but I'm sure mom and dad could not afford the treatment. Financial strains deepened in the house as more and more medical bills came funneling into our lives. I didn't play basketball or try to see Derrick. The hurt and embarrassment kept me away. The whole town knew what happened and we were too emotionally drained to care. Derrick's mother was a nurse at East Orange Hospital and I'm sure word got back to her about my house. I was convinced she told Derrick to stay away for his own safety. I buried thoughts of everyone, Derrick, my brother and my parents. I needed to do that one thing that Alex talked about, getting organized. For starters, I ran every morning to North Orange Park and shot foul shots for one hour. Afterwards, I went to school and stayed to myself except for Candy and Bonnie. They were with me for the long haul and didn't give a rat's ass who was talking about me. That gave me comfort to get through the rest of the school year.

By early April, there were rumors that the school was closing. There wasn't enough money in the budget to support academic and fiscal operations for another year. Parents were scrambling to find a new school for their kids. Candy and Bonnie's schools were chosen quickly by their parents. Candy was going to Good Counsel in September and Bonnie was going to St. Vincent's. As for me, my parents did nothing because they were emotionally immobile. But the coach from St.

Amelia's all girl's prep school in South Orange heard about the closing and she sought me out by the end of April. We had a short-lived run in during my eighth-grade championship basketball tournament. Coach Joan was so impressed by my defensive game that she asked my parents to consider St. Amelia's when I graduated eighth grade. My parents refused the offer realizing that they could not afford the tuition. This time Coach Joan would not let my parents say no. She gave them academic scholarship information since I was in the top ten percent of the Freshman class. There was enough scholarship money to keep me in school for the first year. The only thing I had to do was to get a part-time job to help out with the tuition balance. Wayne Valley High closed without major hoopla. We signed books, took pictures and cried like we were graduating from high school. I didn't care because I knew that it would not change my relationship with Bonnie and Candy. We planned to hang out on the weekends and talk on the phone everyday.

By May, I landed a job at Roy Roger's on Central Avenue in East Orange. My father was so disgusted with my choice, hoping that I would get a job in an office. Little did he know that it was the perfect job for me to clock out and catch the bus to Penn Station. I didn't want to cause any friction in the house so I kept my room clean and kept up with my summer reading list for St. Amelia's. I knew I wouldn't like the school but I did it anyway for fear of getting in trouble or getting my weekend travel privileges taken away. Sometimes I worked a double shift just to have extra cash in my pocket. The first double shift was one I shall never forget. An unkempt man came in one night, nodding out in different directions on my line. Even though there was a shorter line he chose to stand on mine. By the time he reached me I was revolted by his stench and sight. He had four missing front teeth, a pasty substance in the corners of his mouth and oozing cold running from the inner pockets of his eyes. It was ninety degrees that night but he wore a full-length wool coat with holes ravaging every side. He picked his head up to stare at me for a brief second. With his shaky right hand, he threw his pocket change on the counter and said, "Yeah, uh, uh, uh…, lets see now…, uh, uh, let me get, uh, uh, yeah, a tea with six shugahs."

I was revolted by the sight of him, especially the pasty spit flying on the counter. Better yet, I had to pick up every coin he threw at me to count for the drawer. He came out of his stuttering stance and said, "Damn baby, you, you..., you look like that fine ass actress, damn, I forgot what her name was."

I was so disgusted by him that I cut him off and said, "Here is your tea sir, have a nice day, I need to help the other customers."

He got my drift, but wasn't happy that I was rushing him.

"Hey, you don't have to rush me baby, I'm gonna sit right here at my table and make sure nobody messes with you."

Oh, great, just what I needed, a druggie for protection. After that, it seemed like every time I worked, Quadir came for his tea. He also sat at the table that was close to my register. He never spoke to me during the shift, but he stared a hole right through my uniform. There was nothing I could do because he had the right to be there. He annoyed the hell out of me because he reminded me of what my brother would look like in twenty years. I couldn't click my heels like that chick on TV. I needed to be out and having a good time just to escape my world. The best place to do it was the ultimate dance club, the Paradise Garage.

Beyond Control

As long as Derrick was off studying, there was no place for me to release my nervous energy. Sometimes I gorged and kept the food down by running up and down the sidelines of the basketball court at the park. I had to wait for the weekend to dance at the Garage. It was my greatest release of any kind of energy. I had to dance; I needed to burn off my feelings for Derrick since he wasn't around. I danced with guys that looked like him and were built like him. Dancing at the Garage was like having sex with your clothes on and it was the greatest form of expression for a girl like me. One of the managers always let Candy and I in for free even though we were minors. They didn't sell alcohol, but there were other recreational activities to keep a person happy. I stayed clean all the time. My brother was a constant reminder of what drugs could do to a person. He was my anti drug campaign simply because I hated who he had become. I also detested any guy that smoked or drank. That's one of the reasons why I loved clubbing because at least you had the right to say no without someone slipping you a mickey in your drink and then taking advantage of your womanhood before you were ready to give it away. I wore baggy jeans, combat boots, a cut off white tee shirt and my father's army belt. The more I danced, the more my jeans sagged around my waist. If they dropped to the floor, it was a good night because Larry played every cut I loved. One guy that I danced with before came up to me and we started a mini circle on the floor. He took a container out of his pocket and threw the white powdery substance on the floor. Without a fatal slip, the best dancers hit perfect spins on the floor, especially in Chinese slippers. I got lost in the music and forgot about everything from Quadir to my dreaded new school. The musical getaway was the two-pound weight loss that I needed because I binged out on a three piece and two biscuits the night before.

Candy and I closed the club with the maintenance crew at 7:00 am. Larry spinned his ass off and we loved him for it. On the way back to the station, we stopped at a coffee shop and talked to some heads that were at the club with us. It was a great way to compare notes about the songs he played and what celebrities showed up to party. I went back to Candy's house for a quick shower before work. There were no messages from home waiting for me so I went straight to work without incident. Of course, Quadir came stumbling in around six that night to purchase his usual bid. I was exhausted from partying the night before and with three hours left before my shift ended, I was in no mood to listen to his bullshit. Quadir was in rare form like someone or something was bothering him. He actually went to a different register for a change and I was more than happy to have someone else pick up thirty-seven cents off the counter. In fact, I was so happy I ate another three piece and four biscuits. My monthly was well on its way and I was on a salt and sweet binge. I poured honey all over my chicken and saved the buttery biscuits for last. I washed it down with a large diet Dr. Pepper.

By eight-thirty, business was down, so the manager let me leave early. I was glad because the biscuits and soda were damn near sitting in my throat. I forgot to bring my bus schedule so I had no idea what time the bus was coming at South Clinton Avenue and Rhode Island Avenue. With less than two blocks to go to get to the bus stop, my feet were throbbing in raw pain. They were hurting so bad I never noticed three guys walking behind me until one of them heckled at my decency.

"Hey girl, you got a nice piece of ass, can I get some?"

I turned my head to look at them and then kept walking. The unknown face in the middle tugged at my duffel bag and said, "Hope you got some condoms in that bag bitch."

My heart started to sink to the floor in fear but all I could think about was that word bitch. I turned around to face them as Nemesis stood on my shoulder. She had my back all the time, especially when I had PMS. I looked them up and down with sheer disgust and said, "Who you callin' a bitch, you punk ass Mother Fucker."

Even though I could be as fearless as my brother, the words meant little to the three aggressors. The middle light skinned kid clocked me dead in my nose sending me to the ground bleeding. The pain resting in my feet went numb and manifested in my nose. I cupped my hand over my nose as the blood ran down the side of my face and into my earlobe.

"Yeah, I got your bitch right here," he said, as he held his crotch. The ugly one on the end yanked my duffel bag off my arm and threw it behind him on the ground. Then he grabbed me by my arms and started dragging me by my wrist while the other one grabbed me by my ankles. The light skinned kid pulled out a knife and said "Scream bitch and I'll cut the mother fucking shit out of you."

I looked in every direction for an escape route or a passerby, but the street was desolate. Why did it seem like I was getting ready to be attacked by at least one person I knew? My face started to strain and tears swelled in my eyes. Should I scream? Why the hell did I wear chinese slippers to work? Please, someone help me! They started to carry me towards the empty school parking lot. Thank goodness I was a solid girl. Their faces began to strain as they tried to carry me into the parking lot. They were walking so fast and awkward that the uneasy movement started a chemical reaction in my stomach. Buttery biscuits, greasy chicken, honey and cola came together in my throat like creamy caramel mixed in a dumpling bile. I hurled it out like Linda Blair in the Exorcist. The punk bastard who held me by the wrists dropped me like a rotten fish on a hot sidewalk. My right elbow crashed to the ground absorbing my top heavy fall.

"Damn you nasty bitch, you got that shit all over me."

I hocked up the remaining vomit and shot it right at the beast holding my ankles and it landed on his hands. I started laughing at him because he was acting like a little sissy. The perpetrator was revolted by me and threw my ankles to the ground in disgust. But the third one that I didn't see too well kicked me right in the ribs and I finally released the scream that I could not find before. From a dizzying and painful visual distance, I could see the bus seventy-five yards in front of me. My resistance became stronger and I heard a familiar voice yelling at my would be attackers.

“Y'all better leave that girl alone, Little Nate, I'm gonna tell yo momma I seen you bother that girl!"

The three attackers took off running like a bunch of wounded hyenas. I screamed all the way to the bus stop looking like a wounded mad dog frothing at the mouth. An elderly woman stepping off the bus saw me and turned to alert the driver.

"Honey, are you all right?" The old woman extended her hand to help me board the bus. I was panting and aching in every crevice of my body.

I took the first empty seat I could find because the onlookers were shocked at the sight of my tattered clothes. Blood was pouring down my face and seeping into my uniform. Chunky bits of vomit riddled my shirt. The old lady followed me back on board and pulled a nasty tissue out of her pocket. She stood over me in sheer curiosity and concern. All the other passengers sat up to see the commotion as one yelled out, "You know them boys were up to no good the way they scattered away." "Did anyone hurt you, do you need the police?"

For some strange reason, I got defensive like it was the old lady's fault.

"Leave me alone granny, those punks tried to mess with me last week."

She was startled by my wild remark and walked towards the exit.

"Well, I was only trying to help."

"Yeah, well I don't need your help." The passengers on the bus gasped in shocked. I don't even know why I acted like that, but at least she left me alone. The bus took off at the green light and all I could see was Quadir, the unknown voice in the night rummaging through my duffel bag. Another thief rifling through my possessions, never to be seen again. I breathed a sigh of relief that he saved me from those punks but did he have to go through my shit like my brother? The only thing worth taking was a five-dollar bill and a pack of gum. Luckily for me, Quadir had better night vision than I did and knew the kids in the neighborhood. So if it saved me from a good beating or sexual assault, he was no longer a strung out druggie in my eyes. He was a guardian angel in disguise. By the time I got home, I reenacted the scene in my head at least one hundred times. I was angry by the time I put the key in the door. I convinced myself not to tell anyone, especially my parents. They had so much financial worries on their minds and I was sure to get in serious trouble for not acting more responsibly. Sure dear brother was away, but it wasn't worth waking up poor mom and dad. They were going through enough pain and grief without having to worry about me and my story. Besides, I didn't want to ruin my chances of traveling alone at night. So I went to bed without telling them or anyone else who may have cared about me.

I went to work the next day without incident. Surprisingly, my bag and all its contents were returned to the store manager. I looked for Quadir to give him a free tea and a biscuit but he never came. At the end of my shift, I told the manager that it was my last day. I caught a Westlande cab home with the five dollars Quadir never claimed. I sat in the back of the cab with the duffle bag resting on the seat beside me. The bag had a horrific odor emitting from the inside. I opened up the bag, barely realizing that all the places my bag had traveled engulfed all the smells of my experiences in one comatose vapor. I took all of my contents out, paid the driver and left the smelly bag behind. The trauma from the night before finally crept up on me and I needed to let everything go. I got in the shower and cried for my cruel thoughts of Quadir, a kind soul that risked his life for me and who was decent enough to return my duffel bag. I cried for my brother and I cried for the sake of crying. I went back in my room and laid across the bed. Mom and dad were in the other room watching the Jeffersons. They were giving me the royal silent treatment. With everything that happened to me, it was a perfect opportunity to be silent.

On Monday, I got a call from the coach of St. Amelia's. She wanted me to drop by the school and meet the principal, Sister Rose. Rumor had it she had a reputation as a tyrant with hair whiter than Coach Mahoney at St. James. I didn't care because I figured I wouldn't have to deal with her that much. I joined a pick up three on three at North Orange Park and then walked to St. Amelia's. It was at least ninety degrees and I was sweaty and unkempt. I rang the doorbell of the prestigious school and a small boned woman answered the door wide eyed at the sight of me.

"Are you lost young lady?" She looked me upand down like I was Oliver Twist. I shrugged my shoulders holding my basketball under my hand and said, "I'm supposed to see the principal, uh, Sister Rose I think is her name..."

The little assistant barely let me finish and ushered me into the library for a chat. She looked at me with a stern look on her face.

"You do realize that all of our candidates meet with Sister Rose wearing a dress or skirt."

I looked at her like she was crazy and said, "I don't own a dress or a skirt and the coach didn't tell me all of that."

She replied with a disappointed brow, "Oh dear, you must be that Shanelle girl from Wayne Valley High."

"Hmm," I thought to myself. "This is going to be interesting."

Just then, a tall, wiry, white haired woman came into the library frowning at me. "Are you Shanelle?" the crude woman asked. I put together some manners and said, "Yes ma'am."

"Don't you ma'am me young lady, you will address me as Sister Rose, now stand up and look at yourself in that mirror over there right now."

I looked in the direction she was pointing to and noticed a full-length mirror. I looked back at her and said, "I don't need a mirror, I know what I look like."

She walked up to me and confronted me face to face.

"Well I'll tell you one thing, you better enjoy your summer because if you think you're going to come back to my school looking like the wild animal that's standing in front of me now, you will be thrown out of here so fast your mother's head is going to spin."

I kept staring at her eye to eye, clearly she was not finished. "I really don't want you at my school, but Coach Joan, the name you should be addressing her by, is the one who wants you here. You may have had good grades at Wayne Valley, but you're at the bottom of the barrel here. You have a nasty attitude and I heard from a reliable source that you never gave your teachers an ounce of respect, especially Mr. Crollin... Oh, don't think for a minute that I didn't make a few phone calls about you. Tell your mother to call me before August first, your registration has been suspended until she makes the first deposit. Now please leave."

The look on her face was the reaction I had on my face when Quadir walked up to my register for the first time. I went back to the chair I was ushered to and picked up my basketball mumbling, "I don't need this shit."

I bounced my basketball down the hall while the office doors slammed behind me. I didn't care if she heard me or if she told my mother, St. Amelia's was way out of my league. I walked the long way home bouncing my basketball every two steps. On the third step, I pretended to take a jump shot to strengthen my upper arms and to reinforce the strength in my battered and bruised elbow. I blocked out the speeding cars and buses on Scotland Road and headed up Crescent Avenue. By the time I got to the intersection, my hair was drenched and my arms were exhausted from the work out. A car from behind me beeped as I crossed the intersection but I never bothered to look. I could sense that the car was pulling up along side of me, but I still refused to look or give the harasser my time or attention. But when the male voice spoke, my heart began to flutter.

"Hey, number thirty two, can I get your autograph?"

The driver side opened and my handsome black prince stood up towering over his vehicle. I screamed his name out in pure relief and excitement, "Derrick!"

He walked to the front of his car and stretched his arms out smiling ear to ear. I dropped my basketball and jumped into his arms squeezing him tight. Derrick squeezed me back and I was glad he was used to sweat because he didn't react to my damp and sweaty body. He picked me up off the ground and squeezed the life out of me.

"Ahhhh, damn girl, are you happy to see me or what?" I couldn't answer him because holding him was the right release I needed as I buried my face in his neck. I missed him and needed every inch of him as the tears started to fall down my cheek. He pushed me away to see my face and then grabbed me again, this time stroking my hair.

"Shanelle, what's wrong baby girl, you look like you've been in a fight and I thought you would be happy that I surprised you?"

"I am happy to see you, I missed you so much. Look at you, you look taller and smarter. Meanwhile my life sucks!"

Derrick started laughing at me like I was some drama queen. "Girl, c'mon and get in the car."

He put me down and escorted me to the passenger side. Like the gentleman he was, Derrick opened the passenger door and waited until I got in before he closed the door. He got in on his side and I was almost on top of him I sat so close. He started laughing when he put the key in the ignition.

"Girl, your life just keeps on going in crazy directions, what happened to your elbow?"

The white gauze pad covering my hideous scar stood out like a sore thumb.

"It's a long story, I don't want to waste your precious time on lil' 'ole me," I said in my Butterfly McQueen voice. "Let's stop by my house so I can take a quick shower."

Derrick gave me a familiar wink from the past and said, "Are you sure you want to do that?"

I nudged him with my good elbow and said, "I'm positive and besides, you wouldn't want to mess around in my house."

Derrick made himself comfortable on our old living room couch. I hated when company came because we were stuck in the seventies and living in the eighties. Daddy always said our furniture was considered antique but I wanted to haul that stuff on a flat bed straight to Sanford and Son's old junk yard lot in Watts, California. Even if Derrick noticed the worn out furniture, he was too polite to crack on me and my family. I ran upstairs to get ready and jumped in the shower. I rinsed the sweat out of my hair and brushed it back wet in a tight ponytail. I put some baby oil on the surface to give it extra sheen in the hot sun. As I rinsed off, I envisioned myself in an all white outfit. My new white pumpkin seeds, white linen walking shorts with the matching short sleeve top. Silver bangles and my silver hoops. I toweled off, put some lotion on my ashy knees and slid into my outfit. It fit perfectly even though I had a healthy dose of water retention. Walking everywhere and practicing kept my weight manageable. I had a healthy tan at this point so I put on my Maybelline Dial A Lash and a touch of lip gloss. I looked in the mirror and an old friend came to visit.

"So, off on another rendezvous with 'hit it while you can' Derrick?"

I tapped my lips to dull the gloss and ignored the little jealous one. She wasn't happy that I ignored her.

"Oh so you think you're grown now huh?" Got your life all

figured out, like you and Derrick are going to play house somewhere. Get real, you're just a kid to him, a play thing."

I shut my eyes tight to think her away. When I opened my eyes I looked cute and ready to go. I ran downstairs and showed off my new outfit. He didn't seem excited at all by the sight of me this time. He was looking at all the family pictures on the fireplace and in the wall unit.

"Is this your brother?"

He pointed to his early high school days at North Orange High. Nemisis came back in my head, "Yeah, he's studying that psychology and disorder shit, maybe he thinks you're crazy too."

I looked at him yearning for him to pay attention to me this time. I grabbed his arm and pulled him away from the used to be happy memories.

"Yeah that's him let's go, he's not here anymore anyway."

Derrick was surprised and curious.

"Yeah? Where is he?"

I grabbed his wrist and pulled him out the door.

"It's a long story and who really cares where he is as long as he's gone."

I slammed the door and looked at the battered lock. I pushed on the door to make sure it was locked. I still had a constant fear of dear brother finding an escape route and on the way home, plotting his knife attack on me or my mother. Derrick opened the passenger side door and said, "So, where do you want to go?"

It was already two o'clock in the afternoon and I wasn't sure where we could go so I said, "I don't care, as long as I'm with you baby."

Derrick got in on his side and said, "There's a West Indian festival in Brooklyn off of Atlantic Avenue, let's get out of Jersey and hang with some of my people." I laughed and gave him my rendition of a fake Caribbean accent, "Ahh, dem your people heh?"

He laughed and said, "Girl we all dem people."

He put the key in the ignition as fast as he completed his sentence. He usually gave me a little look or a wink, but it didn't happen. All I could think of in that instance was the final song in Cooley High. I forgot the words, but I felt like that was going to be the theme for the evening.

Driving to Brooklyn with Derrick was a great getaway. The hustle and bustle of the people from the view of his car was exciting. I was used to taking the train into the village so a view was another great way to watch people go by hand in hand. Derrick talked about his classes and was engrossed in molecular biology, human psychology and physics. Thank goodness there was visual eye candy to get me through his conversation. He mentioned that there were only a few black students and the ones that were studying with him were nerds. That got my attention because I wanted to know if any girls, or women caught his eye. He was disgusted with my question. "C'mon Shanelle, I said there were hardly any of us and you know I don't swirl."

"I know, I know, but there's going to be a whole lotta chocolate girls in North Carolina studying just about everything and everybody."

Derrick started laughing like I was one of his boys and forgot he was with me.

He replied, "Oh you know that's right..."

I cut him a look from the corner of my eye that could have cut him in half.

"Aw girl, don't look at me like that."

My mouth was wide open ready for a response.

"No see, you forgot you're with me instead of Mookie and Ricky, I swear you guys are all the same and trust me, I'm not a girl."

My remark didn't even phase Derrick. He looked at me and replied, "Shanelle, don't start. I told you I'm not like those nuckleheads out there, but don't think I'm not going to look or..."

I couldn't bare to hear him finish his sentence so I covered my ears like a little child.

"Save it for your homeboys, besides, sometimes I don't know if I'm going to save it for you."

Luckily a red light was in front of us at Church Street and Chambers.

"Are you trying to tell me something?"

I looked out the passenger window to avoid his question and to think of a good answer at the same time. There was a woman tying a balloon on her child's wrist so it wouldn't fly away. The little girl looked at me and I made a funny face at her to make her smile. She smiled back just as Derrick pulled off towards the entrance of the Brooklyn Bridge. I turned back to see if the little girl's mother tied the string successfully, but from the little girl's pathetic teary eyed face and wide mouth, the balloon had escaped her mother's hand and went sailing upward into the sky. I turned around and looked at Mr. Wonderful.

"No, Derrick, I'm not trying to tell you anything except that people grow up, and move on without any strings or feelings attached. I know I love you and I want to wait for you, but I feel like a little kid in your grown up world of physics and microbiology."

He was just like the balloon just set free from the little girl's tiny wrist. The slightest force set it free and flying into the unknown wind being swept through life's challenges and guilty pleasures. We were at the base of the Brooklyn Bridge merging with the oncoming traffic.

Derrick looked annoyed but calm and said, "Girl, I mean Shanelle, you know I can't pull over and grab you up for a Kermit hug because I know you need one right about now. I don't know if all of this is about you, or me, or us, but everybody goes through life feeling the same way you're feeling right now, even me. I feel way out of my league studying all this advanced material but I know that it has purpose in my life and it just feels right. As for you being in my life, I never said that you had to stop your life for me, but I know that I love you and wish that you were the one girl who could share this with me when I'm finished school. Maybe that's not what you want to hear but it's the truth and that's all I've got to give you right now."

Tears started swelling in my eyes again as I absorbed what he had to say. The water below the bridge looked so clear and tranquil as the sun took a temporary rest. Derrick took his hand off the steering wheel and put it on my lap.

"I still love you girl and I always will no matter who we end up with in the future."

Funny, the same thrill that used to send me into a passion pit seemed mildly warm this time. I locked my hands into his as Derrick made a left hand turn on to Atlantic Avenue. I stared out the passenger window and said, "I'm glad you're my friend, but I hate not being able to know you as my lover."

He squeezed my hand back and said, "I'm glad you're my friend, but the time is not right for us to be lovers."

I fought back the tears that wanted to fall and stared out the window. Everything around me was changing, but it felt like it was changing for the worst. In just a few short months Derrick and I seemed to go through a crazy metamorphosis. I thought to myself, "How could something so pleasurable on a stormy winter night change into a slight attraction?"

I don't know if it was me or Derrick going through some life cycle, but with all the color and splendor of the Caribbean festival, we both knew that we were not the same anymore. We walked through the festival holding hands and admired all the beautiful children with painted faces and feathery junkanoo costumes. We shared a five-dollar curry chicken dinner and licked each other's fingers under a splendid oak tree that offered us plenty of shade. There were lapses of silence as we kissed and caressed each other like old times. Derrick stepped on my beautiful white pumpkin seeds and turned them into a tracked shade of brown. I started to get angry at him and I got him back by smacking him in the head as we laughed under the sleepy sun. I sat behind him for a while and whispered fake molecular equations as he laughed and caressed my ankles. He left for a minute to buy some sweet Goombay punch someone had on sale direct from Nassau. We ate cotton candy under the tree and shared the sugary substance with long French kisses. An old man broke our romantic stride and sat down with us for a game of dominoes. We played three hands with the skilled old Trinidadian who beat us mercifully. I kept looking at Derrick, the skilled competitor, thinking how mature he looked in such a short time. We shook hands with the old man and took a seat on a park bench and watched some Brooklyn girls jump double dutch. One of the girls turning the rope took pleasure in spinning her end of the rope faster to mess up the jumper's stride. The chunky buttercup girl proudly announced, "You're out!"

Derrick and I laughed as he bellowed out to the girl, "Hey, you're cheating, you should be out!"

I stepped in and turned the rope to keep the game fair. The chunky girl took a turn and in fifty seconds she was huffing and puffing as the ropes went over and under her head. She finally dropped to the bottom as her friends chimed in, "You're out!"

We all laughed this time as the chunky girl took the rope from me. Derrick took his keys out of his pockets and gave me a look like he was ready to go home. All I could think about was the chunky girl's two words, "You're out!"

I looked at him long and hard while I brushed off the back of my linen shorts. He held out his hands and I extended my hand for our last and final date together. He didn't need to say we were coming to an end, I could just feel it in my bones. The ride home from Brooklyn was long and quiet. The traffic was so backed up to the Brooklyn Bridge, the radio became our buffer. By the time we reached the Holland Tunnel, Derrick got back into a half way decent mood.

"So what are your plans for the rest of the summer?"

I wanted to give him something to think about so I said, "Oh, just working and clubbin' on the weekends."

I cringed at my answer. It sounded so childish, but that's all I could think of to say to him. Derrick looked at me quickly for eye contact and then concentrated on the New Jersey traffic.

"Every weekend?" Derrick asked.

"Well I didn't plan on you being around, it's almost August."

Derrick stroked his hair to the front and then to the back in frustration.

Worry seemed to consume him. I don't know if it was the pressure from studying or me, but something deep inside wished that he would ask me to go with him to North Carolina. I looked out the window and wondered thoughts of being his young housewife while he finished school but that wasn't on his mind.

"I'm leaving on August 10th for North Carolina."

I looked at him hoping he would reconstruct his sentence.

"What did you say?" He turned the radio down and cut off the air conditioner.

"I'm leaving August 10th Shanelle."

"Well good for you Derrick, have fun."

He was surprised by my answer and said, "Damn Shanelle, I'm sorry your life isn't going the way you want it to be, but there's nothing I can do to help you. It's not like I can take you with me girl, your father would have me arrested."

Whatever else he had to say rumbled through my brain and faded to black. I felt like smacking him but I didn't want to crash. I started screaming at him, "Derrick can't you see I need to breathe and I can't! Everybody is after me trying to get whatever they can and I can't take it anymore. I don't know where to go or what to do with myself."

My throat started to swell up with saliva and I started choking as the tears started streaming down my face. "I'm tired of crying, I'm tired of cleaning, I'm tired of running when I should be sleeping."

I paused to catch my breath. "Sometimes I just want to jump off this fucking world and get a damn life refund like a bad batch of cold ass French Fries."

I buried my head in my hands and put them in my lap. There was too much traffic for Derrick to pull over so he drove with one hand and stroked my back. Tears came down like a waterfall. Derrick sped up as I continued to release the pain that was bottled up inside of me. In a muffled voice he listened as I poured myself out to him.

"I don't want you to leave me, I want you to stay. You're the only thing safe and warm in my life. With you, the world is not so crazy and people don't bother me."

I sat up to relieve the pressure in my head and noticed that Derrick passed the exit for the Oranges. I took a tissue out of his glove compartment and said, "Where are we going?"

He grabbed my hand and said, "I can't take you home like this so we're going to stop at Eagle Rock." I took a long deep breath and exhaled.

"That's fine, I didn't want to go home anyway."

We parked at the Eagle Rock reservation in West Orange. The view of New York was spectacular under the evening sky. Derrick put the car in park and climbed in the back seat of his car.

"C'mon Shanelle, lets talk." I climbed over the seat and sat sideways in between his legs. He pulled me in close to him and I laid my head on his chest. He was sweaty with a soft cedar scent. Derrick stroked my hair and said, "What happened to you while I was gone, I was hoping you would just tell me."

He was wrong, like the warrior, I kept things inside like a nasty secret. I opened my mouth to speak. My voice sounded raspy from crying so hard.

"I don't know where to begin Derrick, but so much has happened in so little time."

He held my hand and said, "Girl, your life is like an episode, just start on channel two."

I took a deep breath and thought about what bothered me the most. The first thing that came to mind was dear brother, next was school, then Quadir and last but not least, those punks that broke my spirit the other night. I told Derrick my episodes in it's entirety without any commercial breaks. He didn't take advantage of my weakness by trying to make a move on me. When I got to the story about the guys, I could feel his heart beat build up in a rapid pace. He shifted his body weight upright to hear the rest of the story. He was angry, even though I was able to escape them. He grabbed my face and said, "Did you contact the police?"

"No!" I shouted. "Do you want me to get in more trouble for embarrassing my parents?"

Derrick looked at me like I was crazy.

"Shanelle, don't be ridiculous. This is not about embarrassment! You don't deserve to be treated like that. Besides, your parents are suppose to protect you from harm, not put you in harms way. Look at your life and figure out what you need to do to keep yourself safe. Besides, why didn't you call me? My life is not that important to stop what I'm doing and help you."

I whispered an answer that I wanted him to remember.

"Derrick, I know in my heart that you love me, but the truth is, even though you're here with me now, mentally you were gone. Every time I bring you into my world, I'm weak and while you're gone, I figured I just better tough it out because the chances of us being together are simply impossible."

Derrick's heart rate slowed down again and beat in rhythm with mine. He knew I was right. That molecular world he described could not be combined with restless nights of rescuing lil' 'ole helpless me. I grabbed the sleeve on his jacket and said, "Your life is ahead of you Derrick, go live it, I'll survive, but I have to do things on my own terms."

His car started to stifle me so I climbed back over the seat and got out on the passenger side. Derrick followed as we walked to end of the pathway.

He put his arm around my waist and I crossed my hands in front of me to ward off the slight chill in the air. We stopped at a tall maple tree to finish our talk. Derrick looked at me and said, "Can I still call you?"

I chuckled a little and said, "Sure, as long as my phone is connected." He laughed and said, "If I write, will you write me back?"

"Sure, as long as you send me a stamp."

His last question was our last romantic interlude.

"Can I have one last kiss?"

There was no need to answer him. I closed my eyes and held my face up to him. All I could feel was his beautiful lips on me.

Like that sweet winter evening that seemed so long ago, he slid his tongue in my mouth and made love to my senses. My eyes relaxed more as I released breath through my nose. Derrick whispered in my ear and said, "Remember Shanelle, I love you and I'm coming back one day." One tear of pleasure rolled down my eye. Like those early days in the past, I couldn't speak, but I knew that Derrick and I kissed for the last time. Whether the feelings I had for him were misplaced or misdirected, I knew I could look in the mirror and be proud of that little part of me that was still pure and untouched. A soft breeze got my attention as I started to get goose bumps. I took the first step towards the car and said, "Can you take me home please?"

Derrick, the ultimate gentleman replied, "Anything for you Shanelle."

That night I slept in my clothes while Stevie and Donnie rocked me to sleep. My face was riddled with new and old tears. Tissues were strewn across my bed like puffs of grief and loss. For the moment, my room was finally a quiet respite from the ebb and flow of all the things around me. The last thing I remembered was holding onto Kermie and thinking about tomorrow.

St. Amelia's

Before I could blink it was time to start my Sophomore year at St. Amelia's. We couldn't afford to buy a uniform, so Mrs. Viv bought a Butterick pattern and made two uniforms tailored to my size ten frame. Even though I weighed the same, my legs, arms and butt seemed to take on a new personality. The only good thing was the absence of dear brother to heckle my appearance. He probably would have dubbed me a line backer from the Pittsburg Steelers because my size and my uniform did little to flatter my shape. Orientation for transfer students began at 8:30 am. Many of the girls on St. Amelia's basketball team knew I was coming from Wayne Valley and were ready to initiate me into their morally filled world. I walked through the front door of the school with an attitude. My first assignment was to pay for my registration, books and tuition. Mrs. Viv damn near cursed Sister Rose under her breath as she handed me the blank check.

"Shanelle post date this check for Friday and if Sister Rose has any questions, tell her to call me."

Yeah, stick me with the dirty work. I didn't care anyway, I was hell bent on raising Cain and then getting kicked out. I walked into the office and gave the check to the secretary and said, "Hi, as you already know, I'm Shanelle Brown, the transfer student from Wayne Valley, my mom said you can fill out the check and deposit it today. So sorry it's late, we had a death in the family."

The secretary looked up in complete remorse.

"I'm so sorry to hear that honey, who passed?" I looked at her with puppy dog eyes and lied with a straight face.

"My dog was hit by a drunk driver Labor Day Weekend. His body was splattered all over our street and I'm just now getting over the loss of poor Kiko." The secretary gasped in horror. "Oh dear, I am so sorry to hear that, if you need to talk to Sister Rose during these difficult times..."

"Yeah, that's cool, where's the auditorium?"

The secretary was startled by my lack of remorse.

"Down the hall to the right." I walked out and headed for the auditorium. Once inside, I sat down in the first rear seat. Only trouble sits in the back and Sister Rose was ready for me.

"Girls, as I stated before, we have one new student entering the Sophomore class and I would like you to welcome her. Inger, can you come to the front and welcome Shanelle?"

A tall girl stood up with knobby knees and walked to the front and said, "Shanelle, can you please come to the front so we can welcome you!" I walked to the front, head held high with a large Las Vegas chip on my shoulder. I could hear the heckling as I walked by each of them.

"Stuck up bitch, look at her, she thinks she's cute."

Another comment followed from the middle section, "I can't stand those Wayne Valley Girls, that defunct ass school."

I looked up at Inger and smiled at her with pure evil conviction. She extended her hand and said, "Here at St. Amelia's, we pride ourselves in school spirit and academic commitment."

I shook her hand and whispered in her ear, "Well I guess I won't be hanging with you girlie."

She gasped in disgust while the audience applauded. I rolled my eyes at her and turned around to greet my enemies. They clapped with condescending smiles as they held their heads high. But among the crowd to my delight were some visual she devils who looked like me, slightly homeless, horny and ready for some juvenile delinquency. By lunch time, I was sitting with one of my visual cohorts. She was kind and honest about my time at St. Amelia's.

"As long as you stay out of Sister Rose's office, you should be okay. If you don't, she'll find a way to make your life miserable." I shook my head like it was my first day in the pen.

"Cool, I already had a run in with her in the summer, but thanks for the advice."

After school I had to go to basketball practice to meet the team for early try outs. As I expected, they were all waiting for me taking foul shots in the gym. One person that caught my eye was an arch rival from grammar school. Her name was Lisa Thompson, a five foot seven power forward from East Orange. We played against each other during the summer league games at Metcalf Park and never in my wildest dreams did I intend to play on the same team with her. She had a mean baseline shot that was unstoppable and she loved to talk about my big "box out" butt. She was no way near Portia's popularity or sexual prowess, but she was a drop dead gorgeous Guyanese beauty queen with natural curly hair imported direct from Indian and Chinese DNA. I thought I was going to get attitude from her, but she threw the basketball to me like it was an ice breaker.

"Take your shot at the top of the key number thirty-two, that's still your shot right?"

I caught the ball and put it in motion sending it straight into the net. She got my rebound and threw a chest pass back to me.

"Happy to be here?" I sucked my teeth and replied, "Does it look like it?"

Then her playground wit kicked in like the good old days in the summer league.

"Well if you don't like it here, they could use you in the cafeteria to open up a few cans of peas with those shark like teeth you have."

The other girls on the team started laughing. I started laughing too because she was funny.

"Yeah, I got your can of peas Lisa, real funny."

After that, the girls on the team came up to me one by one and shook my hand to welcome me to St. Amelia's. A long sharp whistle broke up our introduction. It was the coach and she was ready to get us in check.

"Let's go girls, I want ten laps, no slackeys in my camp. Shanelle, I need to see you."

"Already" I thought, so far so good and I was planning on being rebellious. Coach Joan looked me straight in the eyes and broke the bad news.

"Sister Rose wants you to sit out this season because you need to be up to speed with the rest of the girls, especially for algebra. There's nothing I can do except to say that she will allow you to practice with us for strength and conditioning until you try out next year."

I stood there for a minute staring at her in disbelief. How could she do something like this to me? I was excited about playing basketball and that was the only reason I got into this school. The coach continued.

"I already talked to your mother and she agrees. Besides, she thinks it would be a good idea if you helped out in the cafeteria to defer some of your tuition costs."

"Oh hell no coach, I didn't come here..."

She interrupted my sentence and yelled at me in her Boston accent, "Look Brown, I don't know what your problem is but you better get that chip off your shoulder real quick. Nobody's going to feel sorry for your little tantrums, and I'm not going to put up with that mouth of yours." I immediately headed for the exit doors and yelled, "Well then don't, I don't need this shit anyway,"

As I busted through the door, it hit Sister Rose in the stomach sending her straight to the floor gasping for air. All the students ran to her aid and protection.

"Sister, are you all right?" One corny bench warmer patted her brow with a St. Amelia's basketball towel. She was out of breath as she got up but firm in her conviction. "Young lady, apologize for running and march straight to my office for a detention slip and three demerits."

All of the students surrounded her like a sick case of group collaboration. Lisa was the only one that remained neutral. I was new to this system, but it was important to act stupid just to fit into a click. I think I said something stupid like, "What's a demerit?" That question brought frustration to her temples.

"Get out of my face now Ms. Brown."

I backed down by walking back to the office and said out loud,

"Sure, not only did you call Mr. Crollin, I think you ate him too."

Sister Rose replied, "That's going to cost you another demerit and a five page paper on respect."

She was determined to have the last word. I couldn't help but try to get the last word in too and finish off our verbal fist fight. I turned and looked at the other students who appeared shocked and perplexed by my behavior. I winked at Lisa, smiled and said, "Ok, I'll be sure to interview Aretha for the research paper."

Although she didn't answer back, I knew I made a critical mistake that worsened my time at St. Amelia's. Despite the strained relationship with Sister Rose, I managed to sustain three friendships at the school. My most memorable friend and confidant turned out to be Lisa. We were connected in fierce competition and leadership. I confided in her on some of the things that happened to me over the last two years. She was sympathetic to my cause, but in no rush to have a sleep over. On a bright spring day in April, the confidences I shared with Lisa ultimately spared my life a second time. I was sitting in chemistry class riveted by the big white chart of abbreviated elements. Sister Rose's voice came in over the loud speaker exclaiming, "Good afternoon students, will Shanelle Brown please report to the office."

I thought to myself, "Gee, what did I do now?"

I walked out of the classroom and spotted Lisa. I asked her to walk with me to the principal's office and she was curious enough to follow. Thank God she did, because at the top of the landing stood Sister Rose and a shadowed figure in the vestibule of the front lobby. Sister Rose smiled at me and said, "Shanelle, you never told me you had a brother." As the words spewed out of her mouth like a slow motion black and white movie, the figure stepped out of the small vestibule and into plain view. In Lisa's eyesight, she could tell it was the sibling I had described in the past. Lisa's next step would have taken her to the top landing but she reacted quickly and turned around in the opposite direction. I quickly turned to meet dear brother's cunning face as he spoke to me with his mind, "Ah haa, who ever the cutie is, you told her about me and I'm going to have to kill her too."

Sister Rose grabbed my arm and guided us to her office for my final casting call.

"Your brother and I have had such a lovely conversation about you and your activities here. He's been so busy with his printing business, he's had little time to concentrate on you, Shanelle."

I tried to open my mouth but my eyes were shifting to my brother's hands and his khaki pant pockets. I was waiting for the knife to expose itself and slice me with horrific intensity, but dear brother had other thoughts reserved for later. He finally spoke and we all listened as the slightest echo of police sirens came from the southern distance of Scotland Road.

"Actually Shanelle, I locked myself out and was hoping you could give me your key." His voice was calm and assured, but I couldn't help but notice the methodical twist of his right thumb rubbing along his pointer finger. He capped off his sentence by bending his head slightly to the left as if he was studying a heart soaking in embalming fluid. His sentence was met with a strong constitution this time, "Give me the key Shanelle."

I opened my mouth to spew out a lie but I could not take my eyes off of the exposed metal in his pants. Suddenly, four squad cars appeared in the school parking lot, from Sister Rose's window, the secretary opened the door of the office as Steven made a mad dash past her. I started screaming not knowing which one of my classmates he was going to hold hostage for the key to the house. I yelled in terror and frustration, "Help, help me God, he's going to kill us, please help us!"

I fell to my knees as four police officers entered the office. They had their guns drawn and ready to release their fire power. The sight of it caused the little secretary to faint, not withstanding hitting the cherry wood coffee table in Sister Rose's office.

"Is everything alright Sister, we got a 911 call regarding an escaped psychiatric patient."

Sister Rose put her hand over her heart and said, "An escapee, dear God in Heaven!"

The police were determined in their search.

"Where is his Sister?"

Sister Rose couldn't answer. Her face was pale as a ghost. She looked at the blood oozing from the secretary's head and gathered her senses.

"Shanelle, go get Mrs. Ryder and tell her to tend to poor Alice."

Just then Lisa ran in and hugged me in relief.

"Are you alright, did he hurt you?" Sister Rose was not concerned about my safety and welfare.

She screamed at me and said, "Shanelle, go and get Mrs. Ryder right now!"

That innocent accident cost me three years of pain and agony at St. Amelia's. Countless suspensions, demerits, failing grades and intrinsic messages plagued my time there. I was at the bottom of the barrel academically and socially, just as she predicted. I bullied and teased girls until the day I graduated and Sister Rose was definitely glad to see me vanish. With a clear conscious she beckoned me to her office an hour before I received my high school diploma.

"Shanelle Brown, you're a disgrace to human kind and I hope I never see your face again in this lifetime. You have done nothing but spoil and taint the beautiful halls of this fine institution. If it were not for a few people, who for some odd reason see potential in you, I would have thrown you out of here the day you walked in here like a tramp from Forty-Second Street. When you accept your diploma, smile graciously and don't say a word. Don't do a boogie down dance or try to entertain the proud parents seated in the audience who have spent considerable time and money giving their daughters the best education possible. Your parents are seated in the third row, look to them for inspiration, Lord knows nothing inspired you here."

She breathed a sigh of relief and looked at me for a response. I turned my back and walked out. I didn't owe her a thing. I was finished with St. Amelia's and Sister Rose's wicked ways.

Time Flies

Summer came and there was incredible excitement in the air. Out of all my friends, I was the first one to get my driver's license. Everyone was counting on me to get it because we knew it wouldn't be long before it got hot enough for the beach season. I passed my road test with flying colors and my short skirt distracted the driving instructor from the minor mistakes I made. I called my girls to tell them the news and it seemed like the planning began. Candy called back first, "Ok girl, you know we have to get some new bathing suits and get ourselves in shape."

I laughed at her calculated plan. "Girl, you are the bug out! I'm trying to find a way to get the car now, bump the beach. Well maybe not, I've got to get to Alex if he's still there."

Candy started laughing, "Girl, that was so long ago, do you think he'll be there this summer?"

"Oh hell yeah, it seemed like Belmar was his second home. Anyway, I think I'm just going to run small errands for Mrs. Viv so she can start giving me the car. By the end of June we should be straight."

By all accounts, I was right. I gave Mrs. Vivian a break from grocery shopping, trips to the mall and I even took her to visit dear brother in the hospital. He was relocated to a secure facility with little opportunity to escape. The trips in the car were quiet respites for her. She rarely spoke on the way there or on the way home. I can't imagine what she was thinking, but I know that the love she had for Steven was immeasurable. We all had a place in our hearts for him, but for Mrs. Viv the grief was like a slow pendulum of hope then disappointment. His recovery and relapse strained her physically and emotionally for many years and her stoic nature didn't allow for small talk. She only prayed that her dear son would come through this anguished dilemma and live a normal life. I dropped Mrs. Viv off at the hospital and took a quick trip to the mall. Candy was there with one of her soon to be ex-boyfriends. Poor sucker didn't know it, but we did. The beginning of the summer was a good time for a break up, especially since Candy was planning to go to airline school to become a flight attendant. She walked up to me just as I was about to buy my favorite chocolate chip mint ice cream on a sugar cone.

"Sure you want to do that Shanelle?" I laughed as I turned around licking the savory cold mint cream.

"Positive girl." She took my cone and licked the other side. I snatched it back and said, "Damn, I would have bought you one, I don't know where your mouth has been." Candy shifted her eyes to the direction of Macy's. "I'm here with big head and I can't wait to leave, he's getting on my nerves. Oh, listen, I'm going to my cousin's wedding this weekend with my mom down in Asbury Park, if you want to go."

The look on my face appeared disinterested but it was probably going to be the last time I went out with my girl since she was going away to school in two weeks.

"Sure, I'll be your date. What are you going to wear?"

"I think I'm going to sport my black pant suit, but let me know what you're going to wear Shanelle, because we're not going to wear the same thing this time." We were together so much that we had to discuss outfits to avoid looking like twins.

Our fashion trends were in complete unison and we had to be careful about our adult image.

"I think I'm going to show some legs this weekend, just to celebrate the summer. Probably my fuscia jacket and matching mini skirt."

Candy gave me that "excuse me," look.

"Ok, that sounds cool, but don't forget how bad your feet are going to hurt when the party's over."

"I'll take my chances, Asbury sounds corny as hell and I'm sure there won't be any cuties there."

I checked my watch and instantly thought about Mrs. Viv.

"Oh snap, let me get out of here and get my mother, I'll talk to you later."

Dummy finally walked up to Candy and put his arm around her. The sound in her voice was sheer aggravation.

"Bye, call me."

"Ok girl!" I didn't look back and headed for the car to pick up my mother. She seemed relieved to see me and happy to get in the car.

"How's he doing?" I asked. The look on her face went from happy to annoyed in one second flat.

She replied, he who?" She hated when I referred to family members in a "he" or "she," category so I corrected my sentence.

"How is Steven?" She sighed and looked out the passenger window. I looked at her oddly because for a minute, I thought I was looking at a mirror image of myself.

"Ma, did you hear what I said?" She snapped out of her own daydream and said, "Oh, yes, Steven is going to be ok, it's just taking time."

She wiped a small tear that streamed down the side of her face. I turned on WNJR to soothe her emotions on the way home. We stopped at Shopright for some ice cream and a loaf of bread. I was doing everything to keep Mrs. Viv at peace from the sadness she felt even though she was trying to be strong. Once we got home, Mrs. Viv let me take the car and I headed to Candy's house. I took the long way because the car made me feel like I had so much freedom. I hung a right at Grove Street and cut in front of the Grove Street bus. I caught that bus so many times my head started to spin, but I was grateful those days were long gone. Driving gave me so much freedom that I never wanted to take public transportation for as long as I lived. I pulled into Candy's driveway and beeped the horn. Leonard came out to greet me with a smile.

"Where you headed today kid?"

"Hey Pops, nowhere special, just hanging." Leonard was a caring man and always tried to let you know he was something back in his day.

"Drive carefully and don't get sassy with that car out in the street, times are not the way they used to be."

Another lecture, but I didn't care, with the engine running and a new club tape, it was worth it. Candy and I went downtown to Persuassions and bought two more outfits. We bought Jordache jeans, size six for Candy and my usual size ten. I looked in the dressing room and it seemed like my body was changing. My waist seemed slightly narrow and my ass filled out the back of my jeans. I thought I could squeeze into an eight, but Candy assured me that Jordache was not cut for girls like us. It didn't seem to matter that much because I liked the fit. We left Persuassions and hit the Academy Fish Market and split a shrimp and whiting dinner. We loved that spot, especially when they changed the oil. The fish and shrimp were always fresh and it was enough for us to eat without feeling full. On the way home, we pumped some club music and stopped off to pick up some cigarettes for my father. That was always a good way to keep the car. If he didn't have a need to pick up a pack of smokes, we could surely keep the car longer. We went into the house and I took the cigarettes upstairs to my father. He was lying in the bed with the comforter up to his neck watching Soul

Train. Dear daddy worked so hard, up to seventy hours in the week, he surely needed to rest. I gave him the cigarettes although I hated his nicotine habit. There was no problem keeping the car, as long as I gassed it up at the end of the night. It was my senior year and I knew he understood my need to be free. He coughed out loud trying to muffle the sound as he warned me to be careful of other drivers.

"Make sure you get the oil checked too." I kissed him on the forehead and said, "Ok daddy, I'll see you later."

I knew that whenever I called him daddy his big ole' heart seemed to melt. He called me from his room.

"Shanelle, have fun and tell Candy I said hey."

He never said hello to most folks, he usually greeted them with a greeting of "Hey, how are you doing."

Everyone loved him, near and far. He was a loving father and a true friend. On the way downstairs, the phone rang. Candy picked it up because she knew my father never answered and Mrs. Viv was outside talking to the neighbor. As I reached the landing, she handed me the phone. A look of disconcertion was on her face, "It's your brother..."

I took the phone with a smirk on my face.

"Hello." I was cautious, he was joyous.

"Hey, hey Shanelle my Belle, what's going on, how are you doing?"

My response was clear and calculated. The doctors told us to be upbeat and positive when he called. His lucid memory was a good way for him to control his fits of anger against us when he was aggressively psychotic.

"Steven, it's good to hear your voice, never mind me, how are you doing?"

I winked at Candy as she giggled in the palm of her hands.

"I'm just coolin' and making good progress, they're thinking about letting me out by May."

"That's great, I am so happy for you, do you want to speak to dad?"

Dear brother avoided conversation with dad at all cost.

"No, put ma on the phone."

I pointed to the door so Candy could get Mrs. Viv.

"Ok, I'm getting ready to go out, I'll try to stop by and see you next week."

The tone in his voice changed, he knew I was lying. "Yeah, whatever."

Truth be told, I never entered that hospital once nor did I plan on going. I hated hospitals and any thoughts of One Flew Over the

Cuckoo's Nest was enough for me. I threw the phone down and headed for the front door. Candy was right behind me planning our next move.

"Hey, let's go to the Village. Leave the car here and let's take the Forty-Four. We can come back around nine and you can drop me off home."

"Sounds good to me and I want to get some earrings."

The spontaneity in our friendship was so smooth and in sync we barely had disagreements about what to do on any given night. We laughed the whole way to Penn Station, plotting our lives out for the summer and what Candy would do once she got to Pittsburg. Candy had it already planned that she wanted to go to airline school. I knew I was headed straight to Bloomberg College because it was the only college that accepted my pitiful application and transcript. They had a dormitory and a cafeteria and that's all I cared about for the time being. Freedom wasn't too far away and I couldn't wait for September to come to move on campus. Sometimes the laughter stopped between us because we knew our lives were rapidly changing. Since Candy had no interest in college, my stories were one sided, but she listened. I listened to her talk about airline schools and we talked about all the free trips we would take together. Our conversations felt different, but we still had a bond. We promised each other that no matter what, we would be there for each other. The bus arrived at Penn Station and we walked arm in arm off the bus like two silly schoolgirls. She was like the sister I needed in my crazy world. Saturday came and it was time to get ready for the wedding. I felt good as I got dressed. The house was quiet except for Sinbad, who was our new six month old rambunctious mutt. I sat at the mirror and applied pink eye shadow and lipstick. I took my time doing my hair in a simple French roll. I decided to wear pearls to look more mature. It was just the right touch with my French roll. Feeling complete, I grabbed my purse and went downstairs. The full length mirror was the last check and everything looked cool, especially my legs. The phone rang but I chose not to answer it because Mrs. Viv was in the kitchen. She picked it up and greeted the caller. "Yes, how are you Dr. Levitz?" The horn beeped and I was out the door to greet Candy and her mother. I was curious about the call since she had just come from a visit with dear brother, but I dismissed the thought knowing that I would hear about it later. The ride to Asbury was long but the Parkway traffic was light despite the beach traffic. Candy's mother was infamous for not showing up at the church so we went straight to the reception. I was happy because the long drive made me incredibly hungry. Candy touched up her lips and passed the compact back to me to do the same. We gave each other a bid of approval and headed up the stairs to the reception hall. The lobby was filled with crystal and mirrors in every direction. We went to the bathroom to tinkle and do a final touch up on our make-up and hair. Candy's mother left us as she rolled her eyes up in the air.

"You two live in the mirror." We brushed her comments off and went into the bathroom. There were three older women inside but one girl looked my age. To my surprise they were friendly and said hello as we all looked each other up and down. The oldest lady looked at Candy and said, "You must be on the bride's side of the family, because you look like Nina."

Candy smiled at her. Trust me, if Nina wasn't pretty Candy would have rolled her eyes at the woman and walked right out of the bathroom. Candy replied, "She's my first cousin on my mother's side." The woman's eyes lit up. "Oh, you have such a nice family, I'm best friends with Nina's mother, Florence."

"Oh," Candy replied, "Florence is my aunt and my mom's sister."

The lady looked at Candy like she was puzzled that Candy thought she wasn't smart enough to make sense of their family tree. The nice woman turned and looked at me and said, "Are you related to the family?"

I replied, "No, ma'am, Candy and I are best friends."

She looked me up and down and said, "Well I think I'm going to play match maker tonight, because my son is in the wedding and I would love for you to meet him."

She stepped into my space and said, "Where do you live?" I was taken aback by her inquiry, but I didn't want to be rude. "I live in North Orange, exit 145 off the Parkway."

She looked disappointed and said, "Girl that's far, but my son loves to drive."

Candy jumped in and asked the ultimate question. "Well is he cute?"

But before she could answer we were ushered out by the hostess who announced that the DJ was about to introduce the wedding party. We scurried inside and searched for Candy's mother. She flagged us down and pointed to two empty seats. I sat down as the announcer introduced the bridal party. Candy sat head to head with me so we could critique each bridal party member. The flower girl was simply gorgeous as she paraded out with the pea head ring bearer who graciously picked his nose out of sheer nervousness. Candy said, "That's my cousin, Shirelle, she just got a print ad with a big clothing store. I can't remember the name of the store though."

We clapped and smiled at the half way cute couple. Candy grimaced and pointed to the pea headed boy, "I don't know who that pea headed boy is, he must be on the groom's side."

We laughed in an unlady like manner as Candy's mother rolled her eyes at us. We didn't care because our loud raucous behavior blended into the applause of the crowd. As the bride's and groom's parents were introduced, I surveyed the room for cute guys. There were none to be seen except two who were under heavy lock and key by their insecure nymph looking girlfriends. They looked so skinny I looked around for some food. There was fresh bread in the basket but the uproarious laughter from the crowd broke my concentration to see the humorous commotion. People were pointing in the direction of the next groomsman as the announcer held the mike up to his mouth.

"Next we have Bridesmaid, Tammy Foster, accompanied by her brother and Groomsman, Alex Foster."

The crowd clapped louder this time for the brother and sister team. I extended my neck to see the duo, especially the groomsman because he was engaged in some comedic act. All I could see was one of his hands in the air as he escorted his cute, but chubby sister. I couldn't see, so I stood up for a brief moment to see what all the commotion was about. By the time I saw him the laughter stopped and all of my breath left my body. Candy hit me in the leg and said, "Sit down, I can't see girl."

I could barely hear her as I stood up straight and gazed at him. I thought to myself, "No, it couldn't be, could it?"

His sister took her place on the receiving line next to the other bridesmaid. Her back was facing me as I continued to stand. Candy, in sheer curiosity stood up next to me as I sat down in pure shock. She sat down again and moved her chair closer to mine.

"What is wrong with you Shanelle, you look like you've just seen a ghost." A tiny smile nestled in the corner of my lip as I slowly began to clap. Years passed between us and there was an innate need for me to become a lady in that very chair. I began to transform into a regal young lady as I crossed my legs and sat up straight. From head to toe he was covered in a black Armani double breasted tailored tuxedo. He was as cute as the day I saw him at Belmar. The tuxedo was definitely Armani and fit him to perfection like a GQ magazine spread. The skylight from the room emitted sunlight directly on his cinnamon skin that I remembered so long ago. Three years did not affect him as he stood motionless in time like the sunny day at the beach. As the crowd quieted for the entrance of the bride and groom, Alex began to survey the crowd with his piercing eyes and within an instant, the fuscia in my jacket and skirt caught his attention. I nudged Candy as air began to clog my throat. He looked at my legs and slowly carried his eyes up to my face. As I watched him survey my appearance, Candy leaned her ear towards me as I gasped for breath. His eyes finally met mine as I breathlessly whispered to her, "It's him."

The look on Alex's face was rhetorical and if I could read his mind, he was thinking, "No way, is that the girl..."

I couldn't finish the thought as Candy demanded to know more. She nudged me with her elbow and searched my eyes for an answer. She replied, "Who?"

I continued to clap as the possible realization sunk into Alex's mind. He slowly started to reveal a devilish grin on his face as he continued to stare. He read my lips as Candy pressed for more information and said, "Tell me girl, who is it?"

As I said his name again, he read my lips from a fifty yard stance and dropped his calling card with a wink, as I said to Candy with sheer excitement, "Alex."

Alex

The groom began to dance with his mother as the bridal party took their seats. After their dance, the DJ mellowed the crowd with some light R&B and jazz. Candy and I collapsed into a frenzied whisper.

"Are you sure it's him?" Candy gripped my wrist for an answer. I shook my head in confident affirmation, "Yes, it's him and he is fine."

I sipped some water to control my nervousness and confirmed my own thoughts, "Oh, it's him alright, I can't believe he is here at your cousin's wedding."

As I put the water back on the table, my glass hit the plate which signaled the first "clang" to get the bride and groom to kiss. Candy took her knife and began to hit her glass to drown out her excitement for me.

"Girl, don't you fuck this one up, he is definitely the one for you."

She started laughing as she whispered in my ear. "His eyes are all over you, look at him!"

I smiled at Candy and surveyed the room in his direction. I was interrupted by the woman from the bathroom. She came over to the table and chatted with Candy's mother about meeting us in the bathroom. The regal lady walked up to me and said, "Well, I've only got one son and he carried on so bad up there, I'm sure you saw him."

Candy jumped right in to rescue me from my bumbling behavior.

"Alex is your son?"

She looked at Candy with reassurance and then turned to me and said, "Yes, that's my boy and I would love for you to meet him young lady."

My heart started to beat frantically as Alex raised his glass in our direction. His mother smiled and said, "Looks like he approves an introduction, but I'll wait until later."

She put her hand on my shoulder as I assembled the table napkin on my lap like I had refined table manners.

"I'm sorry, I didn't get your name sweetheart?"

I cleared my throat and confidently said, "Shanelle, Shanelle Brown."

She looked pleased and said, "Well it's nice to meet you. Don't run away from here without meeting my son okay?"

She embraced my hand like a warm and inviting gesture to her world.

I replied, "Yes ma'am, it would be my pleasure to meet your son."

Luckily I didn't have to wait that long to meet him. Candy made me push my food around my plate and limited me to vegetables and one slice of bread.

"Girrrrrrrl," She said, "You better pick at your food tonight, your prince charming has arrived and I don't need you farting or burping around him. Go to the bathroom and put some lip gloss on now."

She slipped me her lipgloss underneath the table and I made a quick exit. Little did I know, Alex took flight after me and was waiting in the small vestibule when I opened the door to exit the ladies room. I was startled at first but he, in his handsome appearance, soothed me just by his presence. "So, we meet again."

He extended his hand to shake mine and I carefully placed my small hand in his. I was grateful that the reception hall had fresh liquid soap and lotion in the bathroom. My hands were clean and soft as our hands embraced. I looked down at his manicured hands. He embraced my left hand in a strong and subtle manner as goose bumps quickly rippled up my arm. The rest of his skin that was hidden underneath his Armani tuxedo looked firm and appealing. I looked up into his eyes with a coy smile and said,

"Looks that way, huh."

"Uggghhhh," I thought to myself, "Did you have to say huh?"

Nemesis even popped in for a minute, "Listen dummy, he's not looking for an air head so snap out of it, you're acting like Chrissy from Three's Company."

I gathered my thoughts and got organized for our conversation. The moment had to continue because he didn't let go of my hand yet.

"Belmar right?" I asked.

He smiled without showing any teeth like the joker and nodded his head in affirmation as he stared into my eyes. He slowly released my hands and placed both of his hands behind his back and said, "Time sure flies when you think you're having fun?"

"Hmmm," I thought, a play on words, my favorite game. "You haven't been having fun, it seems to me you were having fun when you were playing football with your friends."

He threw his head back like Sony Crockett from Miami Vice and said, "I haven't had a fun moment since you turned me down."

I knew where he was going with this commentary, so I went right along with his little game, "Whatever do you mean Alex?"

I said with a grin. He took one hand from behind his back and motioned an outbound pass like he was holding a football.

"You still owe me a football game on the beach." I smiled showing my pearly whites and said, "Touch, flag or tackle?"

Alex exposed the dimples in his cheeks with his warm smile and said, "Your choice lady."

Nemesis returned and said, "Quite the officer and a gentlemen, ask him what he's been up to over the years, Lord knows you need a handsome black prince right about now."

I blinked her away and said, "I don't want to be rude, but shouldn't we go back inside?"

Alex stepped in closer to me and said, "After three years of hoping to one day see you again without pretty boy by your side, we don't owe the bride and groom anything but a white envelope."

He offered his arm for me to hold and asked, "There's a gazebo outside, let's talk."

As he completed his sentence, Careless Whisper began to play for all the romantic couples. Alex looked at me as he placed his free hand on mine and said, "I won't take no for an answer."

I smiled and looked straight ahead to the gazebo entrance doors and said, "Sure, let's talk."

We walked on to a crimson brick patio. The walkway was arranged with beautiful white lights and white impatients. Begonias were nestled in early bloom in big potted plants that sweetened the scenery. At the end of the pathway, the gazebo was waiting for us to enhance the scenery. Alex escorted me to the white wooden bench and waited for me to sit down before he sat next to me. He sat close at first and looked at the distance between us. He shifted his weight further away from me which tickled me on the inside. My smile stimulated his curiosity and he asked, "What is it, did I do something wrong?"

I abruptly answered, "No, no, you're fine, you're such a gentleman now." He laughed and looked the other way to see who else was outside with us on that summery night.

"Thank you," Alex replied. "Might I add that you have turned into quite the lady?"

He put his finger to his temple as if he suddenly remembered something.

"Before I forget, let me reintroduce myself, my name is Alex Foster."

I shook his hand and replied, "I'm Shanelle, Shanelle Brown."

He looked up into the sky and said, "All this time your name was Shanelle?"

I looked up into the sky and said, "What do you mean all of this time?"

Alex looked at me and said, "If ever there was a time I wanted a girl to runaway with me was the day I saw you on the beach. Trust me, you looked hurt and abandoned, even though you were wrapped up in whatever his name was. When I asked you if you wanted to play, I knew you wanted to leave him and jump into a new challenge. I admit, I was unkind to you, but part of me said give it a try, she may want to meet you after all."

Alex stood up and walk to the gazebo's edge. "Anyway, does it matter now? As fate would have it, you're here and so am I. My mother said that after all I've been through, now is the time to find a real lady. But never in my wildest dreams did I think I would see you again. There was nothing I could do that day except to try to get your name and number when he wasn't looking. I was so fixated on you that I couldn't concentrate on the game. I remembered thinking that I was horrible to you in Dunkin' Donuts but I guess I was jealous that I wasn't the guy that you were with."

I looked at him and said, "Yes, you did say horrible things to me, but you also said things that made sense to me. I wondered if I knew you from a past life or something."

Alex pointed to the reception hall and laughed. Little did we know, we were providing his mother a visual view of our introduction as she sat eating her main course. She smiled and gave us the thumbs up. I looked at him to help him figure out what happened since the first time we met and said, "Well, if it interests you at all, I'm not with him, oh, excuse me, I mean, pretty boy as you described him."

As Alex sat on the bench, he shifted his weight so that his hands were folded in between his legs. I noticed the massive weight in his back and thought about what it must have taken to assemble his wardrobe because he was so muscular.

"Well, whether you were with him or not, when I spotted you sitting at the table, I said to myself, this time, she's not going to get away."

I laughed like he had some nerve. "Oh really, you think?"

He laughed as I looked at his handsome side profile. In a flirtatious gesture, he took his thumb and pointer finger and softly pinched my chin. "No, I'm serious, you're not going to get away this time."

I would have responded but the doors to the gazebo opened and his sister politely shouted, "Alex, you're being rude. I don't care what mommy says, I don't have anyone in there to dance with, so come on right now!"

He rolled his eyes up in his head and said, "My little sister, a royal pain in the ass."

She may have been a pain in the ass but it was enough to break up our interlude. Alex stood up and held his arm out again. "Duty calls, but promise you won't dance with anyone but me." I embraced his arm and said, "I promise Alex." He looked down at me and said, "I love the way you say my name." Alex's chubby sister held the door open for us as we went inside. He politely introduced us, but she was not impressed with the likes of me and my mini skirt. She looked me up and down like a little old woman fanning herself on first Sunday and ushered her brother away. He laughed as he walked down the hall with her and said, "Chill sis, chill, I'm going to dance with you."

He turned around and winked at me again as I went into the bathroom to check my makeup. Candy was hiding in stall number two waiting for the scoop. She jumped out of the stall as I opened the door and scared the living shit out of me.

"Ah Haaa!" Candy shouted as she lifted her arms up like one of the zombies from the Night of the Living Dead.

"Stop playing, girl, you know I hate that scary shit."

Candy didn't care if I jumped out of my skin, she wanted all the details. "Well, what happened, what did he say, did you get his phone number?"

"No," I calmly replied.

"What do you mean no, don't play with me Shanelle."

"I'm not playing, we were talking and he didn't get to ask me because his sister interrupted us." Candy put her hand on my shoulder in support.

"Yeah, I saw chubbyliscious. After she ate she was looking around for a pitiful soul to dance with her. I guess Alex comes in handy for her." I shook my head in agreement.

"Yeah, now she's guarding him like Joe Dumars on Michael Jordan."

Candy laughed like she had a little secret.

"Well Miss Thang, one thing is for sure, little sis' can't give him what you got."

I smiled, but all I wanted was a moment of his time. Just then, Alex's mother came into the bathroom to put the rest of the puzzle pieces together. She brushed off Candy and walked right up to me. "So, you met my handsome son." I looked at her and said, "Yes, he is handsome and we've met." She reached out and touched my upper arms and said, "My daughters are very protective of their only brother, but don't mind them they're harmless."

I was curious about that because Alex didn't have the time to mention other sisters in the short time that we spoke in the gazebo.

"How many daughters do you have?" I asked. She stuck out her chest proudly and said, "I have five daughters and one son, Alex of course."

Candy forgot her manners and congeniality and said, "Damn, you got six kids?"

She gave Candy a stern look and said, "Excuse me, I have six beautiful adult children and I'm proud of each and every one of them, especially my baby boy son, who happens to be a police officer."

Candy was amazed at her fortitude and confidence, "Yeah you seem really proud." She looked at me this time and said, "I ought to be, my husband Vernest and I have been married for forty-two years and have raised some wonderful children. I must admit I'm looking for some wonderful grandchildren about now."

I ignored her grandchildren comments and patted the oil around my eyes and said, "Well, from the looks of things, you've raised a beautiful family, especially your son."

She looked at me with motherly joy in her eyes.

"Well, let me get Tammy off of his back so the two of you can enjoy yourselves. Are you having a nice time? I talked to Candy's mother and she said you were going through some rough times."

My face got flushed with embarrassment to think that they were talking about me.

"Put it this way, with your son, I feel like Cinderella."

She smiled and said, "Child, my son is nothing but a gentleman, so enjoy his company and live your life, you deserve the best."

I don't know how much of that had to do with her son, but Candy's mother could have put a good spin on my dramatic life which may have appealed to Mrs. Foster's kindness towards me. I walked back into the reception hall and took my seat. The last entree was waiting for me, but I couldn't eat. I wanted to frantically get up and search for him but I couldn't find the will power. Candy made her way to the floor to dance to Billie Jean while I nibbled on some bread. The DJ concluded and softly spoke into the mike, "Ladies and gentleman, no wedding would be complete without this song, a special request from the groom to the bride."

I sat up to hear what song he was going to play. Suddenly, I felt someone tap me on the shoulder. I turned and there was my cinnamon vision asking me to dance as the Whisper's came on playing Chocolate Girl. I could have melted right there before the words wooed us into one being. The tall shoes on my feet complimented his height as he held his hand in mine and wrapped the other around my waist. Alex put his mouth to my ear and sang those beautiful words every brown girl loves to hear.

"If there was, such a thing as a wish come true..."

I began to melt in his caress as he changed the words to the song and spoke to me.

"Shanelle, run away with me. Let's take that day back at the beach and make it ours this time. My heart and soul is telling me that tonight is our chance and I'm never going to let you go."

My feet were killing me just as Candy predicted but the pleasure of Alex's words put me on a cloud of sweet unimaginable delight. I wasn't tall enough to whisper so I looked up into his eyes and said, "Let's go."

Alex looked at me and smiled. He pulled me into him until the conclusion of the song. Without saying a word, we separated on the dance floor and made our way back to our assigned seats. I sat next to Candy and hatched my plot in her ear. She was more than happy to hear it as she smiled from ear to ear.

"He's a cop so you know you can trust him. Is he going to take you home?" I looked at her as if she forgot our backup plan. I said, "I'm staying at your house remember?"

"Oh yeah," Candy said as she winked at me.

"Girl, be safe and don't do anything I wouldn't do, which is just about everything."

I laughed and said, "I'll see you tonight."

I picked up my clutch bag and headed for the exit. Alex was standing in the hallway near the exit with his keys in his hands. When he saw me coming, he held out his hands like we were runaway love slaves.

"You look beautiful, if I haven't told you already."

I grabbed his hands with my sweaty palms and headed out the door. I wanted to pique his interest in me so I asked him a question about his car.

"Do you still have that Mazda RX 7?" He looked at me quite surprised and said, "How did you know that?" As he opened the door to his maroon two seater,

I slid inside and said "I watched you drive away that day."

He leaned on the passenger door and looked at me like I had some surprises in my back pocket.

"How very observant of you, are you in law enforcement too?"

I laughed as he closed the door. Alex got in the car and started the ignition. I looked around his immaculate vehicle and smelled the aroma of his vanilla flavored car tree.

"You keep your vehicle in excellent shape Alex."

He looked down at my legs that were fully exposed and said,

"You've kept yourself in pretty good shape yourself, but I'm going to be a gentleman tonight." I punched him in the arm in a friendly gesture and pulled my skirt down.

"I'll make sure you do Alex."

The clock in his car was off by ten minutes but it was eight thirty by the time we reached Belmar Beach. It was a perfect night to be with him as we got out of the car. There were plenty of couples on the beach but none as fine as the two of us. My feet took a heavy toll in his cramped car and they were throbbing by the time we got out of the car. I grabbed his wrist and made my first confession. "Alex, I must say that the only way I'm going to enjoy spending time with you is to get out of these killer pumps, my feet are killing me."

He looked down at my feet and was sympathetic to my cause. "What's your favorite color?" Alex asked.

"Pink," I replied.

"Ok, I'll get you some flip flops for the beach, I'll be right back."

I closed the door and took off my sheer stockings. I opened the car door and let my feet dangle in the cool evening breeze. In an instant he was back with a cute pair of pink flip flops. He took them out of the bag and held them up for me to see.

"How are these?" I didn't care if they were camouflage in color. He was so handsome in his Armani tux, anything he said or did would have been irresistible. He went to the trunk and took out a blanket.

"I always keep a blanket in the car for the beach, let's go sit down."

The image of our first meeting came to mind and I said, "I was hoping you had your football." He threw his head back in laughter and replied, "You're right, you're right," and went back to the trunk for the football. Alex took off his tie and unbuttoned the first two buttons of his shirt as I put on my new flip flops. Thank God I got a pedicure last week, with a skirt as short as mine, I wouldn't be caught dead in such an outfit, but it fit the mood and our questionable plans for the evening. We walked on the boardwalk to a flight of stairs leading to the beach. There were plenty of romantic couples on the beach, so I felt comfortable in our moment. Alex spread the blanket out by throwing it in the air. It landed perfectly the first time on the cold sand. Surprisingly, we were pretty close to the water's edge but the cold sand soothed my swollen feet. Alex sensed that I was in need of podiatry care. He pointed to my feet and said, "Do you mind if I help you with those helpless feet?"

I tugged at my mini skirt and slid my legs down and straight out.

"I trust you, go ahead."

He took his jacket off and placed it around my shoulders, I didn't recognize his fragrance but it was a mature scent that began to fill my lungs and warm my soul. Alex dug a small trench in the sand for my feet and let the water from the tide fill the hole. He didn't remove his shoes and didn't seem to care that they were getting ruined by the wind swept sand and crashing water. He grabbed my left foot and slowly placed it in the sandy trench. The cool water enticed my feet as he gently massaged the top of my foot in small circles. He took my other foot and placed it in the trench. He proceeded to do the same with my right foot. I looked at him and relaxed my entire body. He was so focused on my foot treatment even though he appeared to be this unnatural force of strength and brawn. He sat closer to me and let my left ankle rest on his tailored pants. He didn't care about the sand particles or dust that was forming on his clothes. He massaged the ball of my foot as I bit down on my lip. There was definitely a hot spot there and it was firing up Kitty. I pulled my foot away to his surprise and he reacted by saying, "I'm sorry, too rough?"

I put my hand on his shoulder for support and said, "No, no, it feels wonderful, too wonderful."

He brushed the residual sand off of his hands and said "I'll give your other foot a break then. Leave it in the sand, it's cool enough to relieve some of the pain."

Just as he finished his sentence, the water came too close to us and went right between my legs. I jumped up as Alex reacted to my response.

"Hey, it's just water, let's move further back."

I started walking away from the spot to avoid another rush of cold water. I knew that he was watching me we with baited breath as I headed for the dry sand. "I wish I had some shorts or sweat pants to give you, the store was closing when I bought you the flip flops."

I was so happy he was making such a fuss over me, but I could also sense that he was getting nervous. I turned around to face him and wrapped myself in his scented tuxedo jacket.

"I'm fine really, you're so sweet, let's just sit over here and talk, I want to meet you all over again."

We sat down simultaneously and looked at each other.

I wanted to look away, but I couldn't. The thoughts I jotted down were right in focus as I stared at him. Looking at him forced me into a confession.

"I wrote about you when I left the beach that day."

His warm eyes looked at me in total disbelief. "Stop playing, you were so wrapped up into that guy."

I invaded his space by fixing the collar on his shirt and said, "Alex, I'll never forget it, I wrote something like, your cinnamon vision fires and burns a critical synapse in my brain, make me sane, I want to know your name, or something like that. I have it at home if you want a copy."

He reacted with a shocked look on his face. "Wow you were feeling all of that?"

I laughed because he was enjoying his glorified moment.

"Yes, the entire situation was so mysterious that I had to memorialize you after you told me to bring my big pretty legs back to you."

Alex placed his hand on my knee and said, "And here you are. I can't believe it although I must confess, I didn't write a poem about you, I just played Al Green all night like a pitiful soul. Now that you're here, I'm going to have to play some new songs because I don't want to be that miserable again."

I looked out into the vast ocean and said, "I love music too, what song would you play now?"

Alex looked me in the eyes and said, "Definitely, Luther. "Never too much."

I nodded my head in approval and said, "Yeah, that's a good song."

He looked at me and entered my space again by grabbing my hand.

"Is there any song you can think of Shanelle?"

Honestly, I didn't have any song in my head. I was praying it wouldn't be Cassanova Brown by Teena Marie, because I wanted to wish for the best.

"I'm a poet, but I'll let you know if one comes to mind."

I tried to make small talk before my body chemistry took over. I was definitely feeling Alex and I didn't want to ruin it with my sexually charged virgin ways. I was also surprised that Nemesis didn't visit me during this exchange. I decided to make small talk as I caressed his hand with my thumb.

"So, I understand you're a police officer."

He replied by shaking his head in approval and then licked his beautiful lips.

"Yes, that's correct, it pays the bills and keeps me honest."

"I like honesty, it's a good quality."

He took advantage of my comment and said, "Well be honest with me and tell me why you looked like a girl on the run when I saw you so long ago."

I looked at the ocean and spoke to the open water, "I was on the run and I'm still on the run Alex. I remembered the things you told me but the answers never came. But I'm starting college in the fall and staying in the dorm. Maybe the taste of freedom will set me free."

He put his arm around my shoulders and replied, "Is your mind free or are you physically trapped?"

I looked at the gleaming light over the ocean waters searching for a rational answer.

"I think I need to be mentally free, I will never be physically trapped from anything as long as I live."

Alex looked out into the ocean with me and said, "Believe you me Shanelle, we've all been there, no matter how hard we try, it takes fortitude in the individual to break those mental chains, whatever they are."

I wondered where his philosophy came from and asked, "Are you free Alex?"

He turned from the beauty of the ocean and looked me right in the eye. "Shanelle, I've always been free. Maybe I'm just different, but there's only been a few hurdles in my life that I had to overcome. There's only one hurdle that will follow me until the day I die, but I'm sitting here with you, content with my life and even happier that I'm looking at you again. What more can I ask for except the unknown and when it comes, whatever it is, I'll be ready for the challenge."

I began to get chilly and put my arms through the sleeves of his jacket.

"I'm happy for you and anyone else who feels free. I can't wait for my turn."

Alex let go of my hand and pulled me into him for warmth.

"When you find it or feel it Shanelle, I hope I'm the one that can share it with you."

I relaxed my shoulders and leaned on him with pure excitement and pleasure. The feelings that I had for Derrick were not the same feelings that were beginning with Alex. There seemed to be value and comfort in the things he said to me first. I felt like I could begin to relax and let myself go with him. Not by acting like a wild child but expressing myself with confident liberation. I turned to him and grabbed his face with my cold hands. He looked into my eyes and searched for the thoughts in my mind. I pulled him towards me and softly kissed him on his lips. He didn't seemed surprised as I pulled away to look at his reaction. This time I reintroduced myself and said, "It's nice to meet you, my name is Shanelle."

Alex pulled me closer into his massive chest and said, "My name is Alex and I'm so glad you came back to me chocolate girl."

He brought his lips to mine and released his tongue into my mouth. He tasted minty fresh with a hint of chocolate mint the bride and groom offered as favors.

That kiss seemed to last forever in his arms. I wanted to believe that Alex was all mine without a concocted plan written into a formed script. He dreamed of me and I dreamed of him, there wasn't anything better than that moment in time. His kiss was so tender and he was such a gentleman. He didn't explore me with curious hands and profane expletives. He just kissed me with pure passion and delicate desire. I stopped kissing him for a moment and looked at him to see if he was still with me. For a minute, I thought I was dreaming, but that night on the Atlantic seashore, my shining star connected to my liberation and unearthed vision of a new life simply defined as womanhood. We sat on the beach for two more hours lasting until the sunrise. It was a beautiful sight to behold as we held each other with relaxed and weary eyes. Alex didn't have to work the next day but he wanted to make a respectable woman out of me and gassed up the car to drive me home.

We stopped at a diner on Highway 35 for coffee and breakfast. Patrons smiled at us as we walked in looking like two tussled love birds who lived a night on the beach. We played footsie under the table and exchanged phone numbers. He asked about my college and asked me to show him where it was so he could visit me there in the fall. We talked about his time in the police academy and his experience as the second black police officer in Lakewood. Our conversation flowed rhythmically as the sun took the day hostage. We drove down the Parkway laughing and chatting like two old friends. Every now and then, Alex invaded my space in a charming way. He had a beautiful side profile that kept me out of the passenger window and staring directly at his awesome splendor. We went to Bloomberg College for a driving tour and then headed to Candy's house. We sat outside in his car for another hour and I began to worry about his physical energy because we were out so long. We both slid into our seats and I rested my head on his shoulder. He asked for a copy of my poem and I promised to mail him a copy. His voice sounded sexy and groggy as he promised to call me at the Parkway rest stop. Our conversation revealed that he had his own apartment and that he was single and available. We planned a date for the following weekend and promised to talk every night at his expense. He got out of his car and walked around to the passenger side. I looked up at him and smiled as he assisted me on to the sidewalk. He asked for a hug and I gave in to his embrace. It was powerful and soothing at the same time. I opened my eyes and Candy caught my attention by jumping up and down in the window on the second floor like I scored a touch down. We walked up the pathway and stood by the door. Alex grabbed my chin and held my face up to his and said, "I had a wonderful time Shanelle, I can't wait to see you again."

Alex took a step down so that we were at an even height. He grabbed my chin again in a playful manner and said, "Thank you for coming to the wedding, thank you for remembering me, thank you for the beach and thank you for this kiss."

He pulled my face into his and kissed me with his beautiful lips and tongue. Afterwards he turned around and got into his car. He started up his Mazda and left into the early morning sun. I sat on the steps as Candy came barreling outside. She damn near jumped on my back in complete happiness for me.

"Girl tell me every wicked detail or I'll kill you." Her reaction changed as something flashed in her thoughts. "Oh, by the way, Mrs. Viv called, she really wants to kill you if you don't call home."

I Dream Alex

Candy and I bolted for the stairs so I could take a shower. Our post adolescent screaming was driving her father nuts so he banged on the door for us to settle down. She sat on the bathroom floor as I told her every detail of our time together. She screamed at all the juicy parts, especially our first kiss.

"Work it, work it," Candy screamed.

We gave each other high fives and Candy smacked the bathroom floor during the foot massage scene.

"Hand me a towel and my bag so I can get dressed."

She gave me two minutes of privacy just to get dressed and we crawled into bed for a daytime slumber party. I held the sheet up to my chin as I finished the rest of the story. The phone rang and Candy picked it up.

"Hi...oh, hello Alex."

Candy kicked me with her foot and said, "She's right here hold on." She threw the phone to me like we were playing hot potato. I picked it up and put my sexy voice on as Candy shared the phone's ear piece with me.

"Hello."

"Hi Shanelle, it's me Alex."

Candy pinched my arm as I replied back to him.

"Hi, are you home yet?" The phone sounded hollow as he spoke to me.

"No, I'm at a rest stop but I wanted to let you know that I was thinking about you and I'll give you a call tomorrow."

I was dying to say, "Call me in five minutes, then again and again and again."

Candy gave me the thumbs up to say yes and I said, "Ok Alex, I had a great time, I'll talk to you tomorrow."

I waited for him to say goodbye before I hung up. I handed the phone to Candy like I was a corporate executive.

"Not bad, huh?"

Candy started laughing, "Not bad at all skeezer!"

We laughed under the covers as Candy's father banged on the door again and said, "Y'all quit all that raucous in there, I have a headache!"

It wasn't a headache at all, he was grouchy today and we were going to pay for it if we stayed in the house. I didn't want to go anywhere because I wanted to wait for his phone call. I waited around for Derrick's calls all the time, but this time the rules were going to change and I was going to keep busy. I unpacked my bags and helped Candy clean up the blue room. I didn't realize how exhausted I was until we finished. I plopped down on the bed and was fast asleep snoring into a dream fashioned for me and Alex.

It was five thirty sharp when my darling came home. He threw his briefcase on the cream leather sofa and called for his lovely wife.

"Shanelle, I'm home baby, where are you?"

"Up here," I called, as I applied some Jasmine oil to my legs. He walked into the bedroom as he loosened his Brook Brother's gold pin striped tie. Sensing his need to be free from search warrants and wire-tapping, my sexy CIA agent stood in the doorway staring at his love starved wife. I stood up on the bed to unbutton his shirt and removed his cufflinks.

"Long day sweetheart?" He buried his head in my breasts and said,

"Not with you in my life."

He used his teeth to pull apart the satin bow holding my see through camisole together. I caressed his head as he kissed each nipple in anguished passion. I tried to tell him about my day at the law office, but he was lost in the smell of my skin.

"I made partner today," I said, as my handsome husband continued to nestle in my bosom.

He pulled my sheer panties down and whispered to me, "Well, what better way to celebrate than me being inside of you."

I dug my nails in his back and squeaked his name. "Alex, take me now, my king."

Alex picked me up and laid me on the bed side ways as he surveyed my golden brown skin. He explored every inch of me with his glorious tongue. Then he put his masculine hands under my thick thighs and massaged them into creamy ecstasy. Suddenly, the phone rang. I didn't open my eyes to answer it but I began to think, "We're so in love, we don't own a phone."

A second ring pushed my beautiful dream deep into a

subconscious cranial cavity. Candy pushed my shoulders again and said, "Shanelle, wake up, it's your mother."

I jumped up startled at the thought of my vivid dream. Candy pushed the phone in my hand and said, "It's your mother." I took the phone from Candy and collected my thoughts. There was a strange and empty silence as Mrs. Viv's breath bellowed through the phone.

"Hey mom." I was short and to the point without offering any excuses. My nonchalant greeting begged her response as she beckoned me through the phone.

"Shanelle." She was angry in her tone. I answered her back with an attitude, "What?"

This time Mrs. Viv became indignant, "Don't you what me girl, what is this all about?"

I wanted to annoy her so I replied, "What do you mean what is this all about?"

The look on Candy's face was riddled with confusion. She poked me in the arm with a puzzled look on her face. Mrs. Viv continued her line of questioning. "Do you think our house is a hotel or something, maybe you think you can just check in and check out at your leisure?"

"I never said that mom."

She started to scream into the phone, "Well that's how you're acting and your father and I are not going to tolerate your behavior, you've been gone for two days and not once did you call home and let me know what you're doing."

I was surprised at this sudden concern in my absence.

"Mom, I've been with Candy the whole weekend. This is routine to me and I don't understand why you're yelling at me."

Mrs. Viv took a deep breath and said, "If you plan on living in this house Shanelle, then you need to be accountable for your actions and let your father and I know where you're at, that's what we expect from you."

I got angry and began to pull on the phone cord.

"Expect? That word doesn't come easy for me living in that house. I never know what to expect from one day to the next, so I choose to be somewhere more predictable. Now if I come home today, what should I expect; an argument, the silent treatment, a new bag to pack or what?"

No answer followed my hostile exchange. Mrs. Viv hung up the phone leaving me to figure out the answer. I hung up the phone and put my head in my lap.

Candy rubbed the back of my neck and said, "Girl it's going to be all right and you'll figure everything out." I picked up my bag and gave Candy a hug. "Are you sure you don't want a ride home?" asked Candy.

"No," I replied, "The walk will do me some good, thanks anyway."

Exit Wounds

Even though I had enough money to get home by cab or by bus, I decided to walk home. The three mile hike back to North Orange was filled with so many visual memories of days gone by and days I didn't want to remember anymore. I walked up Central Avenue and passed my favorite fast food joint, the flame broiled smell enticed my need to eat, but I decided not to eat out of frustration. I walked through the park and waved to the same people that were hanging out in the park three days ago with no direction or purpose. I walked past Bennie's Ice Cream Truck and bid his delicious chip candy crunch bar a fond farewell. Even Portia drove by in her new Celica GTX. She rolled her eyes at me as she drove by me but her emotions didn't phase me. I walked past the gas station and headed home. There were a few cars parked in front of the house and I noticed that the front door was open. Even on this hot day, it was unusual for Mrs. Viv to leave the door open. I walked in the door to a host of family and friends gathered around the prodigal son. Once again, he had returned home in true familial style and grace.

A pathway cleared as I stood and stared at him. He was groomed and polished with clear skin. He held out his arms to hug me but I could not bear to receive his embrace. His thumb stroked his pointer finger in the same manner back at the high school. He didn't need a key this time. He was welcomed with open arms from everyone except me. I walked away and went upstairs while Mrs. Viv made excuses for my rude behavior. I entered my room and started to pack a new bag. A few things were necessary to accompany my exit, my driver's license, social security card and acceptance letter. I resigned my village wardrobe and put my pumpkin seeds in a plastic Shoprite bag. New clothes could come my way after a full forty hours of work. In the mean time, Candy wouldn't have any problem lending me a few big tee shirts. Taking a final walk down the stairs, no noises or whispers followed me. The squeaks in the stairs were the regular sounds an old house resonates after years of growth and passage. The look on my face was not deserving of commentary from Mrs. Viv. I think she knew I was checking out for good. I closed the door behind me as curious family members peeked out the window to follow my path. Without question I was going to take the bus back to Candy's house until classes started at Bloomberg College. There was a quiet bed in the blue room and a sense of calm from the roof to the basement. I was going to rest and get organized until school started and without question, it made sense to live there instead of running with the dead. New life came to me that day and adolescence seemed to wash away in my mind. There were new things to think about, including Alex.

Hope

Even though my resolve to get my life together was a priority, there was a constant pull and tug in my heart for my family. Candy's mom and dad let me stay, but a starlight of hope begged for peace in my brother's recovery. I buried the thoughts in my head in order to concentrate on the things that mattered in my life especially starting college in the fall and the excitement for time with Alex. Deep down inside I was longing for his phone call just to hear him speak and breathe. I was excited by his demeanor and hoped that he was the gentleman his mother described him to be back at the reception. It was one full day since I saw him and I needed to feel the magic of last night again. I helped Candy carry a small dresser from the attic to the blue room to hold my personal belongs. We sat on the bed and plotted out some last minute job prospects before school started. Even though I needed to take out loans, I also needed money for books and clothes. The thought of how I was going to manage made me think about food so Candy and I walked to Toni's Pizza and shared it with the family. I washed the dishes and swept the kitchen floor. Candy's mother was grateful for my help and offered me some apple pie. Candy topped it off with some vanilla ice cream and the flavors mixed together washed my worries away. As we were cleaning up, the phone rang. Candy's mother answered it and I noticed she began to smile as she talked to the mysterious caller.

"Yes, she's here, hold on please."

Candy's mother handed me the phone, "It's for you," she whispered, "It's Alex." Candy poked me in the butt and pushed me towards the phone. I wanted to speak to him without Candy leaning into the phone. Trust me, I loved her to death, but I needed to be secluded from the world while I listened to his intentions. I handed Candy the phone so I could take the call upstairs. I climbed the stairs three at a time in my need to speak to him. My heart beat in rapid rhythms as I thought about what he was going to say to me. I picked up the phone off the floor and cleared my throat before I spoke and said, "Hi Alex."

Alex sighed with relief and said, "Shanelle, is everything ok? I called your house, but I think I may have had the wrong phone number."

I dreaded to think what happened as the food in my stomach began to make me nauseous. I found the courage to reveal the embarrassing situation and asked, "Why, what happened, who did you speak to?"

Alex said, "A guy picked up the phone and when I asked for you he started whispering in the phone like a phone prank or something and said, 'Shanelle is dead asshole.' After that he hung up on me. He thought it was funny, but I didn't, who was that?"

Alex was furious and I was sick to my stomach as the food began to instantly spoil. There was silence on the line and I didn't know if he was going to be forgiving. Empathy changed the tone in his voice as he asked, "Shanelle, who was that on the phone?" I wanted to be angry at dear brother's long range attempt to spoil the things inside of my stomach and my head. I felt angry and embarrassed, but I felt honesty was my best defense. I immediately apologized to Alex for my brother's cruel behavior towards me and said, "That sounded like my brother, but it's a long story."

Alex became more empathetic and said, "Shanelle, you don't have to apologize, but that was messed up. I would never do that to my sisters."

"Rightly so," I thought, but Alex was no Steven, nor was anyone else in the world. I leaned back to settle the swelling in my stomach. Even the thought that dear brother was getting this much attention all the way across town made me sick. Although I was comforted by his call, the shame of hiding secrets shamed my existence. Pressure filled in my neck and shoulders as forced air filled my lungs and throat at the thought of this constant unannounced humiliation. I forced the embarrassment down my throat and changed the subject. I closed my eyes and listened to Alex's calm breathing pattern as I began to slowly take in his calming energy. My heart began to race again with dizzying euphoria and I thought I was going to faint. I couldn't make sense of my anxiety so I sat down and rubbed my stomach. I was aroused and anxious at the same time and I needed to relieve this feeling of anguished euphoria. I asked Alex to hold on and I went to the bathroom. I turned on the faucet and let cool water run down my fingertips and into my cupped palms as I rinsed my face off. The cold water sharpened my intensity and made me focus on the things that complimented my life. I wiped the watery residue from my face and went back to the phone call I so needed. I thanked Alex for holding on and changed the subject to put his worries at ease.

"So," I replied with calm enthusiasm, "I'm alive and I've been thinking about you."

I didn't sound pretentious or anxious, I was glad he called and I wanted him to keep calling me, so I had to make him think my life wasn't as flawed as I appeared some three years ago. Besides, I wanted him to call forever and a lifetime and I was determined to make it happen. The pause between us forced him to finally speak.

"Well, I am more than happy to hear you're living and breathing and I would love to see you again if that's ok with you."

I sat on the bed and leaned back on the pillow as the food slowly began to settle in my stomach. I closed my eyes and pictured his dark brown skin and piercing eyes.

"Sure," I replied, "I would love to see you again." The thought occurred to me that he was a police officer, so I inquired if he had to work. He was amused by my question.

"Ah, you like a working man? Well yes, I do have to work, but most police officers have rotating shifts. So I work four days on and then I have off for two consecutive days. But don't worry Shanelle, I won't let my thoughts of you make me lose my job, but there's going to be some tough days ahead if I can't see you. You've been on my mind since I left and I didn't want to leave. I don't have to go back to work until Tuesday so help me think good thoughts before I go back to rounding up the bad guys."

With innocent and decadence combined, I replied, "Don't forget the bad girls."

Alex laughed in a sexy way and said, "No bad girls here, but I'll make an exception for you if you try to escape." I twisted the phone cord around my finger sending it into temporary paralysis.

"Well, let's not get into that right now Officer Foster, when do you want to get together?"

"Well," Alex said, "I have two days off and I would love to see you both days."

My mouth gaped open as my pointer finger became numb.

"The entire time? Alex, you live so far and I don't really know if…,"

Alex interrupted me to protect his masculine pride, "Shanelle, leave the driving up to me. I'm used to driving for long periods and I'm in Essex at least twice a week for narcotics training. But don't get the wrong impression Shanelle, I'll bring you home both days." His commitment to meet my needs warmed me inside and settled my stomach as I rubbed it in downward strokes to entice the digestion process. "Ok, just tell me what time you want me to be ready." I began to melt as I released the phone cord from my asphyxiated finger. I crossed my legs like a lady in bloom and waited for his answer.

"Three o'clock?" Alex asked.

"Sounds great," I replied. "But what do you want to do?"

There was a brief pause as I began to caress the phone cord by stroking it up and down.

"How about dinner and a movie?" Alex said. I smiled and replied, "Dinner and a movie would suit me just fine." Alex paused and said, "I'm glad you're smiling again."

I was perplexed because I wondered how he knew.

"How did you know that?" I asked.

"It doesn't matter Shanelle, what matters is that I make you happy." My smile widened as I stood up and paced the floor with the phone in my hand. I thought of the day we first met and remembered how arrogant he was towards me and said, "I like who you've become Alex."

Alex paused and said, "Yeah, me too, change is good Shanelle, I'll see you at three, okay?" I stood in the doorway and leaned against the frame and said, "See you then."

We hung up the phone as I paused to reflect upon our conversation.

"Yes, change is good Alex," I thought as I looked at the clock.

With less than two hours to get ready, Candy needed to invade my space for a much needed makeover. I wanted our date to be perfect so I called Candy from the stairway landing. She came upstairs ready to take on any mission that needed her attention. I shouted from the top of the steps as she ran upstairs.

"Girl, Alex wants to see me today in two hours!" Candy immediately abandoned her plans for the evening and transformed into a fashion designer and consultant.

"Ok," she said, "Let's think, I know, you need to wear all white, something crisp, clean and pure."

I didn't have any new clothes to wear, but there was some left over wardrobe in her closet. Candy pulled me into the blue room and closed the door. She looked in the closet as she fell to the floor scrambling for bags shoved in the back of the closet. She took out a bag from Joyce Leslie's and said, "Here, I bought these pedal pushers for you last week but you need them now. Wear my sleeveless mock tee shirt with your white pumps and sailor cap."

I took off my clothes and put the pedal pushers on to preview the ensemble. We walked to the full length mirror and stared at our creation. I thought my legs looked heavy but my white pumps made me look leaner. My shoulders began to sag as Candy pushed my frame in an upright position. She comforted me by saying, "Shanelle, you don't look fat so don't even say it, you look nice." I turned to see my side profile and smoothed out the roundness in my stomach. Candy stood in front of me and held my chin up with her hand. "You're not fat Shanelle, you're just shapely and Alex would not have looked twice if he wasn't interested."

I thought about what she said and how much her personal attention meant to me. A small grin came into being as I looked sideways again.

"You're right," I replied, as I remembered that December day with Alex. With a dreamy look at my lean legs I said to Candy, "Do you remember what Alex told me?"

Candy popped me in the back of the head and said, "You've said it a million times, take the Parkway South to exit 98 and bring those big pretty legs with you, gosh Shanelle, you are so damn conceited, I swear."

She smacked the fatty part of my thigh and said,

"Girl, just remember I brought you and those big legs right to Alex, so when you two get married, don't make me wear an ugly dress with goofy ass ruffles because I'll kick your ass."

We laughed so hard, I didn't realize how much time escaped. I looked at the wall clock and said, "Girl, I have an hour and a half to go, let's hurry."

In signature class and style, I jumped in the shower, washed my hair with Cream of Nature Shampoo and Conditioner. Candy passed me her St. Eves facial scrub and cut some cucumbers for my weary eyes. I rested for five minutes while Candy applied facial moisture to my face and neck. I sat in front of the full length mirror as Candy oiled my damp scalp and brushed my hair back. She put some Nunile along my hairline and donned a scarf on my head to keep my wavy edges down. She took out her makeup bag and I opened my case. The theme for the evening was light and romantic. She went into her room to get her Safari perfume as I applied a light foundation. I curled my eyelashes with my eyelash curler and whipped my eyelashes into shape like the baby doll eyes the guys loved me for. I wanted Alex to see passion in my eyes so I put the dial all the way up to ten for a thicker look. I waited until 2:45 pm before I put my matte pink lipstick on. Candy put some gel in my hair and I put on my sailor cap. We sat on the bed and chatted as Candy gave me a quick manicure and then dried my nails with a blow dryer on a cool setting. We stared at each other once or twice and giggled as the momentum to Alex's arrival stirred to a boiling point. We sat on the bed and looked at Cosmopolitan magazines. We were expecting him to beep the horn at three o'clock but there was no sound. Candy looked out the window to see if his car was outside. As she pulled the shade away from the window she shifted her eyes back to me like a private detective and said, "Mazda RX 7 right?"

I squeezed my eyes tight and jumped up and down with pure excitement as I stood up to meet my prince and said, "Yes that's him."

Candy pushed the shade back to the window and looked at me with pure elation.

"Girl, he's got a single white rose and a big ole' brown teddy bear."

We were shocked right out of our skin when the doorbell rang. For a while I stood there in disbelief, trying to convince myself that this could be happening to me. A silence fell upon the blue room as Candy and I stretched our necks out the bedroom door to hear their conversation. The base in his voice sounded so calm and collected as he introduced himself. Candy brought clarity to the moment by patting me on the cheek.

"Candy to Shanelle, Candy to Shanelle, do you read me, over."

I looked at her and then gave her a big sisterly hug for being happy for my new adventure. She squeezed me back and whispered in my ear, "Listen Brown, don't screw this one up. Act like a lady, even though we know you're a brute."

For my own self worth, I took Candy's advice and sauntered down the stairs to the second landing. I could see Alex's shoes in the entrance of the porch as he stood tall and proud. He also checked his watch so I sped up my step and walked to the bottom. As my white pumps touched the living room floor, He focused his away from Candy's father and stared directly at me. I walked up to him as he extended his hand bearing a single white rose. My dark brown cinnamon vision was well suited in a crisp white shirt with small navy pinstripes and navy linen slacks. He looked pleasingly cool and absolutely charming. Alex handed me the rose and said, "One single rose for a beautiful single lady."

I took the rose and held it in my hand like a delicate bird and replied, "Thank you Alex."

Candy sensed my nervousness and took the rose from my hand. "She rolled her eyes at me and said, "Let me get a vase for that flower."

She also introduced herself again because I was in a warm

trance, "Hi, I'm Candy, I guess you met my parents?"

Alex entertained the on lookers as I continued to gaze at him. He only spoke a sentence or two and then looked at me for approval. I raised my eyebrows and smiled at him as he picked up the big brown teddy bear off the patio chair and said, "If you ever need a bear hug, you can hold on to him until I can get to you."

Candy's entire family turned and walked off the porch sensing that things were just too personal for them to be hanging around. Candy mumbled under her breath just loud enough for me to hear and said, "I guess that frog is going right in the garbage when she gets back."

Even Leonard chimed in about how smooth he was and said, "Yeah, I like that cat."

I quickly closed the front door to avoid future embarrassment. When I turned around to face Alex he immediately grabbed my hand and checked my pulse. "Yes, you are alive and you look beautiful."

I looked up into his eyes and hair. Alex's hair was freshly groomed and he was glowing from a clean shave. His chiseled chin and jaw line was all I needed to wrap him in a box and keep him as secret. He took off my sailor cap and held my chin up for a soft kiss. I suddenly became shy as I looked down at his feet. Alex asked me to look at him and said, "Tell me what you're thinking Shanelle, I promise not to bite."

I wanted everything to be perfect for our date and it was hard to find the words to say. So I opened my mouth and said what was in my heart.

"I just want tonight to be perfect for us. I can't stop staring at you, but I don't think I can help myself." Alex put my sailor cap back on my head and said, "Shanelle, you can look at me forever, I'm not leaving unless you beg me to."

I wanted to say more to him, but I kept my feelings inside. I was nervous and my palms were getting sweaty.

Alex opened the door and escorted me to the passenger door. Like the gentleman he was, I didn't have to wait for a prom to feel special. Besides, I ditched the prom because I didn't feel like listening to hillbilly music. Alex opened the door for me as I slid seductively into the front seat. His car was meticulously clean and smelled of citrus fruit. He walked around to the driver's side and adjusted his frame into the front seat. Even though he was a big guy, he looked comfortable sitting next to me. Alex politely excused himself as he reached over to the glove compartment to get his sunglasses. The strength of his arm resting on me aroused me as I began to smell his cologne. Instead of restless nerves taking over, I relaxed and slid down into the seat. Alex put on his glasses and said, "Where to lovely lady?"

His question processed in slow motion as I smelled his cologne lingering in the air. I was completely aroused by the entire atmosphere and I wanted him to kiss me before we left.

Instead, I cleared my throat to focus on my need to keep things as simple as his manner presented. Our clothes were a testament to our evening so I replied, "South Street Seaport."

To my surprise, even though he was from South Jersey, he knew his way around the area.

The drive into the city was pleasant and cheerful. I was so enamored by Alex's charm and conversation that I didn't look at the beautiful scenery around me. He took his glasses off for a while which excited me because the simple gesture allowed me to look deep into his eyes with my own dreamy eyes. Every time he shifted gears he made eye contact with me. I felt pretty and ladylike as I crossed my legs in his front seat. He paid the toll at the Lincoln Tunnel and a pretty brown sister was in the tollbooth to receive his money. She smiled at Alex as she politely exchanged a greeting and gave him his change. Like any real sister who is confident in her own spot, she gave me that look like, "Girl, he is fine, work it, work it!"

As if Paris was really burning, I was working it.

I laughed at his corny jokes and listened to his crime stories with devoted attention. Alex wasn't the type of brother that touched you to emphasize his thoughts. He looked me straight in the eyes like he had a strong constitution. He sought my opinion on everything we talked about. You could tell he had strong family values and a desired interest to settle down and take care of his family. In every subtle way, I intertwined into his conversation my ability to cook, clean, carry kids on my hips and bring home a paycheck. He laughed at my hardiness and my need to challenge him on political points. I didn't feel like he was out of my league when it came to politics and systems, but he did have an experienced based wisdom that was not within my reach. I could tell that he liked my interest in what really mattered in the world. Alex paid for parking as I sat in the car. He held the door open as he put the parking stub in his wallet. I got out of the car and stretched my legs as Alex noticed my white pumps from the wedding.

"Are you going to be ok in those shoes if we walk around?" I started to stretch from the long ride and said, "As long as we don't have to dance I'm fine."

He extended his hand to mine and said, "White shoes and a dance, hmm, interesting concept."

I walked away thinking to myself, "He might just be the one."

The world around us at South Street Seaport looked like people in motion with creative expression and fashion. I wasn't fazed by any of it because I was completely captivated by Alex's energy and wicked charm. We walked into shops and he picked up a few shirts on sale. He wanted to buy me a pretty sundress but I was too embarrassed to accept the retail invitation. All he knew was that I was admiring the full length linen dress so he asked the sales girl to tell me my size and to wrap it up. Now trust me, that's a risky game to play because by the look on her face she looked like she was going to say, "We don't have any size fourteens in stock."

If she did the old Shanelle would have jumped out of my body with Nemesis as a back up and knocked her out. She was in a good mood today exclaiming, "Definitely a size ten sir, we have them."

I turned to look at other clothing thinking, "Act like you know girlfriend."

Alex carried the bags as we went into other stores. He asked if I was ready to eat and although I wasn't, I didn't want to act like I was weight conscious. He even added his own opinion of my size.

"You're in the wrong weight class anyway, I need to get five extra pounds on you."

I playfully smacked him in the arm. That was worrisome to me, because I didn't want to gain weight, I wanted to lose an extra ten pounds. We found a lovely restaurant by the docks and the hostess escorted us to an intimate table in the corner of the restaurant. The ambiance was just what I was looking for as he held a chair out for me. "What a gentleman," I said as he took his seat. Alex was tall so our knees touched under the table when he sat down. He looked me in the eyes and said, "Still happy?"

I turned my head slightly to the side and made myself at home and said, "Yes, I'm happy."

This time Alex lost a touch of confidence and looked down smiling. I leaned over the table and took one of his moves by pinching his chin and said, "There's nothing interesting on the table to look at so look at me and I'll stay happy forever."

The face of a devilish little boy appeared as he held my hand and said, "I like the sound of that Shanelle." Dinner came and Alex and I dined on lobster tails dipped in warm creamy butter. We laughed at the polka dot bibs that brought humor to the atmosphere as he began to feed some to me. Like two children lost in a chocolate factory, we let the wet substances roll down our fingers and wrists. Alex confessed that he was not a drinker and was glad to hear that I was free from alcohol and cigarettes. As he spoke to me he grabbed my left hand and stroked each finger with his buttery drenched fingertips. I began to tell him about my glory days as a basketball player as he admired my garnet ring. He stroked his thumb around the perimeter of the ring and asked, "A gift?" I looked him in the eyes with sincere honesty as thoughts of home welled up in my chest and pounded my heart. Alex held my entire hand as it rested in his strong grip. Curiosity beckoned his next question, "An old friend?" Even if Alex was trying to stir up my past at the beach, my ring offered no clues. I took my hand away and held my own hand admiring the gift that my father gave me so long ago. The answer was easy but the thought overwhelmed my tear ducts as one dropped into my plate splashing into the oil based substance. I looked at him with memories from home and said, "My father gave it to me, it's a symbol of my virtue."

Alex was confused at first but clarity must have come as he thought of his own sisters.

"Ah yes, I get it, did it work?" I wanted to make sure I understood him, and said, "Being pure?" He looked deep into my eyes as I slowly opened my mouth and said, "Yes."

Alex didn't smile or laugh. He took my hand in his and said, "I knew you were different."

I didn't say anything because half of me was pleased with his respect for me and the other half was torn by the family I left behind mentally. Alex handed me a tissue as I patted my face dry. I quietly excused myself and went to the ladies restroom. There was a beautiful oval mirror that caught my attention. I patted my face some more, confident that something good could happen between Alex and myself. I left the bathroom without a need to cry or shove my face into the toilet bowl. By the time I came out, he paid the check and tipped the waitress. The view at the Seaport was so beautiful that night, we didn't want to leave. We found a secluded place to chat at an outside café and shared a slice of cheesecake and spring water. He casually sipped from my cup which said a lot about me and his level of trust. We held hands at the table as I talked about my fall classes. He told me he wanted me to meet his family by going to church with him in the morning. I told him that I didn't have anything to wear but he quickly reminded me that I did by holding up the linen dress he bought me. He wanted me to meet his sisters because they couldn't believe their dreamy brother, by fate, met the girl he was rude to at the beach so long ago. The only one that wasn't too pleased was his baby sister Tammy. They were so close in age, she looked up to him as a role model and was a tomboy all of her life. It was pleasant listening to his love for his family and I was elated that he wanted to introduce me to all of them. I told him that I was surprised that he wasn't dating anyone because he was so handsome and charming but he said most of the girls he knew had the wrong intentions. They were described as the "sit back and see what you can get." kind of girls. He was more interested in a woman who had her own sense of independence and self worth, much like the spirited girl who wanted to play football that day but was held back by the insecure boyfriend.

"Funny," I replied, "He's a memory now and long gone as far as I'm concerned."

Alex held my hand and pressed his thumb on my ring and said, "Let's take things slow."

That suited me perfectly so I replied, "Yes, let's take things slow."

By the time Alex and I finished our conversation, it was ten o'clock and I was getting quite tired. We stood up, stretched and held hands as we walked back to the car. I made myself comfortable as Alex paid for the ticket. He got into the car and offered me a mint before putting one into his mouth. Even in the smallest gesture, Alex was a gentleman and his vibe relaxed my need to be overly provocative. He put the key in the ignition and let the windows down. Alex popped in a Sade tape for the ride home as her sultry voice wooed us back to New Jersey. There was a sobriety check inspection after we exited the Holland Tunnel into New Jersey. Who knows why they did it, but traffic was backed up for miles. The traffic stopped to a standstill and the music also stopped. Alex put the car in park and made our moment special by grabbing my hand. He turned my garnet ring around exposing just the band of gold. I looked at him and searched his eyes for the meaning of his gesture. He stared at the band of gold and looked at me as he stroked the back of my hand and said, "My parents are still together after all these years, I think I know why my mother's simple gold ring means so much to her."

Silence filled his car amidst the evening traffic and blaring lights. I bit my lip like the days gone by and looked at the ground. Alex whispered to me a I searched a place to rest my need for him but he held my hand to his mouth and kissed my gold band.

"Shanelle, look at me," he said, as he caressed my chin in his direction. I looked into his eyes and it felt like my body was going to take flight. Alex pulled his face into mine and kissed me. He stopped for a moment and said, "Tell me you believe in fate Shanelle."

Like a line out of a famous holiday classic, I rattled on like a princess, "I believe, I believe."

The car behind us beeped their horn to signal us to move forward. Alex put the car in drive and moved forward fifty feet. He put the car in park and looked into the rear view mirror to see who the impatient traveler was and said, "Some people have no patience."

It was the perfect opportunity for me to introduce one issue that worried me about Alex. I didn't want to rush things with him but I was scared I was going to lose him if I didn't. Maybe honesty would do me some good right now and if he said no, the pain of him leaving me wouldn't be so tragic. He shifted the car into first gear and I said, "Alex, I need to ask you a question." He seemed curious and said, "What is it Shanelle?"

I shifted my body weight to face him in the car and said, "You mentioned that some people don't have patience, but I'm wondering how long you would wait for me?" I twisted my garnet gem back to it's original position as I waited for Alex's answer. He replied, "As long as you're my lady, you can wear your ring with pride and when you're ready, I'm sure you'll let me know. I mean, let's face it Shanelle, I'm no angel, but I am willing to wait. I must admit, I want to be the one to replace that ring with something else, like a commitment." All of a sudden I became very nervous because I couldn't imagine how the distance between us was going to work. Alex lived so far away and I wondered if he would be true to me. Little did I know that he had the answer figured out.

"I think I told you already, you're different and I'm willing to wait for you. I hope you know that I'm tired of running too Shanelle. I need commitment and someone to be there with me when the chips are down. That kind of love takes time to mature and I want to spend that time with you." I felt so comforted by his words that tears began to roll down my face. I couldn't help myself so I kissed him. He was excited by my touch as I caressed his face and called his name. Alex was a wonderful kisser. His kiss was so inviting and it was the first time that I actually felt a pleasurable sensation in my stomach. Our kiss would have continued if not for the tapping sound on his window. Alex rolled down his window and flashed his badge. The officer stepped back and let Alex ride the shoulder as the officer signaled a clearance sign to the officers up ahead. Witty as it was I said, "Must be nice."

Alex looked at me and said, "Right now, you're nice."

I turned around and looked straight ahead as I wrapped my arms around myself wishing that I was being held in Alex's embrace. He took my sailor cap off and said, "You know what?"

I looked at him as I checked for any loose hair strands as he said, "You've got a Sade forehead girl."

Laughter filled our compact existence as he drove back to Candy's house and I nestled down into the pleasure of commitment. We got back to Candy's house around midnight and it was Alex's turn to plan our date for Sunday. He took the bag containing the dress and handed it to me as we entered the porch. Alex kissed me goodnight and told me that he would come promptly at 7:30 am so we could make it to Metropolitan Baptist in Lakewood. The next morning came within lightening speed and before I knew it I was in Alex's world, engaging in fellowship at his church. Everyone, including Alex's family, was warm and inviting. Mrs. Foster gave me a generous hug as she rubbed my back in small circles.

"You look radiant and I'm so glad you met my son Shanelle. His sisters have been teasing him non-stop, but I think it's wonderful that the two of you found each other again."

After church, we went to a diner for breakfast. A table was reserved for them in the back and based on the waitress's knowledge of the order, you could tell they went there quite often. As I expected, Alex's sister was slightly reserved in her demeanor towards me but to my surprise, after engaging in some idle chit chat with her, we discovered that she played high school basketball. She was accepted to Penn State and had not heard of Bloomberg College. I didn't feel insecure because our common bond snapped her out of her jealousy. Mrs. Foster kissed me twice that day and did everything in her power to make me comfortable. There were stolen moments between Alex and I in the kitchen and in the living room. His sisters shared secrets about Alex's boyhood pranks and opened up the family album for a trip down memory lane. Mr. Foster, the proud father spent most of his time grilling steaks for his family, including six grandchildren of various ages. Alex and I took his twin nephews outside to play tackle football so I finally got a chance to playfully chase him and catch the ball. His sisters admired my tomboy attitude, but Candy would have smacked me for getting sweaty in my long white dress. Alex's oldest sister, Angela, gave me a change of clothes so I wouldn't soil my dress. We drank lemonade and played a fierce game of spades which tested my true ability to be accepted into the family. Papa Foster was slammin' those cards down so hard, I sat the next game out never to return. The game was interrupted by Alex's partner, Jack who called to talk to Alex about work. Alex pulled me into the kitchen with him to receive the call. They exchanged a few secret messages about work and then Alex began to tell Jack about me, "Yeah, she's right here, do you want to say hello?"

I had no idea what they were talking about but I was courteous. "Hi Jack, this is Shanelle." Jack smirked and said, "No kidding, he's been talking about you day and night, and I can't wait to meet you."

I grabbed the phone cord and looked at Alex with admiring eyes as he pulled me in close to him and kissed my Sade forehead. "It was nice speaking with you," I said, as I handed Alex the phone. Alex's mother came from outside with glorious grilled steaks, burgers and shrimp. I was amazed at all the food as my mouth began to water, but I planned to eat like a bird and be the lady that Candy said I should be. Mrs. Foster proclaimed with pride, "Girl, I hope you can cook, because my son can put away some food."

I nodded my head in the affirmative and gave her a list of my specialties Mrs. Viv introduced me to over the years. After lunch, I helped Mrs. Foster wash the dishes and put the food away. Alex told everyone that we were going to leave in order to avoid heavy Parkway traffic. Everyone in Alex's family hugged me goodbye and told me to come back next Sunday. I assumed that I was accepted and Alex confirmed it with a kiss outside.

"They loved you Shanelle, especially my father and once you've got his attention, you're in."

I laughed as I paraded back to his car.

"Are you surprised Alex?"

He grabbed me by the waist and said, "No, but it means a lot to me that you came today."

Alex started to yawn and I noticed his eyes looked sleepy. I felt bad that he had to take another trip back to Candy's house.

"Alex, I'm worried about you not getting enough rest, aren't you tired?"

Alex rubbed his hands through his hair and said, "Shanelle, I'm beat, but I really don't have a choice if you need to get home."

I did need to get home, but I didn't want him to have an accident on the road. Alex shrugged his shoulders and said, "Well, I have to work in the morning. I'll be more than happy to sleep on the couch, but only if you're comfortable with doing that Shanelle. You'll have to find a way to occupy yourself while I'm at work."

I wanted to say yes right away but I knew I needed fresh clothing. He seemed to read my mind as he looked at my new dress. "If you need clothes and stuff, I'll buy you what you need and you can leave them at my place if you want." I took a deep breath and exhaled. I trusted Alex completely and we both needed rest. We drove to JC Penney and I bought some cute panties, a short set and a long pajama top. It was the wrong fashion choice, but I didn't want to entice Alex too much. We went back to his apartment in Lakewood. The apartments were nestled in a gated community with seniors and young couples. Alex greeted many people and introduced me to a few of them.

When we got to his apartment, I was amazed at his simple sense of style. He had a cherry wood wall unit with a matching leather sectional.

His kitchen was hunter green with a natural wood kitchen set. The entire apartment was clean, even the bathroom. Alex threw his keys in a basket and said, "I'm usually a slob, but I have a cleaning lady come in twice a week, just to keep me sane."

I was afraid to put my bags down so I stood in the middle of his living room and waited for his instructions. He was in the kitchen taking water and fruit out of the refrigerator when he realized I did not make myself at home.

"I'm sorry Shanelle, put your bags in the linen closet over there. Wash clothes and towels are also in the linen closet to the left."

Alex washed his hands and wiped them dry as I opened the door to his closet. Alex walked up behind me and said, "Shanelle, make yourself at home and help yourself to whatever you want."

He took me to his bedroom and showed me where I could put my leftover clothes. Afterwards, I washed my dress in his dual washer and dryer and hung it up to dry in his make shift laundry room. Alex turned on the radio to a jazz station and cut up some fruit. I told him I was going to take a shower and he showed me how to use his state of the art showerhead. Alex was quite the handy man and I found that to be very attractive. I closed the door to the bathroom when he left and looked in his mirror. I wiped the residue from under my eyes and used some of my Vaseline to take my make up off. Luckily, he had Cream of Nature Shampoo so I could wash my hair and take a long hot shower. The shower felt wonderful and soothed away all the knots and stress that riddled me throughout the day. I toweled off and put on my pajama shirt and panties. I quietly left the bathroom and pulled my clean hair back into a ponytail. I went into Alex's room and closed the door for some privacy. There was lotion on his nightstand so I took my time and rubbed it into my skin. I was so tired I didn't realize that my need to take a five-minute snooze across his bed, turned into twelve hours of wonderful sleep. When I woke up I was under Alex's comforter wrapped up in the fetal position. I felt lightheaded and incredibly aroused. I looked around the room to focus on the world around me. There were hangers on the doorknob and an empty holster near the nightstand. The nightstand also had a hand written note with my name on the top reading, *"Good morning sleepy head, I was more than happy to see you sleep so soundly. If you need me, page me at 732-5555. Help yourself to anything you need and I'll be home for lunch around 12:15 pm."*

What struck my heart in the deepest way was his farewell which read, *"Falling for Shanelle, Alex."*

I gently held the letter to my face and smelled him. There was a warm hint of cologne on the letter. I rolled around in Alex's bed with the morning sun and smelled his sheets comforter and pillows. He was clean and orderly, well at least the cleaning service kept him that way. I sat up in bed and looked around his room. Every inch of his room was decorated in testosterone. I didn't get out of bed yet because I wanted to read the note one hundred times before I got up. I spoke out loud with the sheets up to my chin, "Falling for Shanelle, Alex."

The sound of it made me wiggle my manicured toes and stretch out in comfort.

"Oh Alex," I thought. "What a wonderful world it would be with you in my life." As I looked around his mahogany inspired room, I noticed the clock on the wall said 10:45 am. "Wow, I can't believe I slept that long."

Alex left the clothes he was wearing the night before on his chair. I wondered when he came into the room and where he slept. I looked down at my legs and I was in the same nightshirt from before. I didn't want to put my short set on until it was time for him to come home, so I put his shirt on and was excited by his natural scent and cologne. I went into the bathroom to survey the damages from such a restful sleep. I was pleased that at least I looked rested. I took a quick shower and washed my hair again for a fresh curly look. I didn't wear any makeup because when he came home for lunch, I didn't want to get any makeup on his uniform. Just the thought of seeing him in a uniform was unimaginable anticipation. I wanted him to come home and break every search and seizure contained in the police manual. As I brushed my teeth, my fantasy took immediate flight.

My dearest Alex busted in the door without a warrant. Hill Street Blues theme music was playing in the background. His policeman's cap was turned around backwards like a homeboy. His shirt and tie was loose with three missing buttons. He was breathing heavily when he walked in with a bottle of cheap wine in his hands. I turned around to my man in blue and said in a coy voice, "What seems to be the problem Officer Alex?"

He walked up to me and handed me a ticket. I read it and the word "GUILTY" was written across the entire form. He picked me up and sat me on his lap while I ravaged his shirt and tie from his muscular frame. Alex stood up as I hung on to him with my big legs wrapped around his waist. He loosened his pants and they dropped to the floor, gun holster and all. He took the cheap wine and poured it on top of my head as the clear liquid ran over my sheer tank top. Alex sat down with me on his lap and surrendered his constitution into me as I screamed with criminal delight. He read me my Miranda warnings as I shouted, "With you, I don't have any rights, take me away!"

Alex handcuffed me to the bed and searched my body for contraband. He used his mouth to subdue me into a plea for help. But there were no public pretenders around. It was just the two of us in our sensual world of bad cop, sexed starved wife.

I splashed water on my face and jumped into the shower. I couldn't possibly have another fantasy because I had to get dressed, clean up and make lunch for him. I only had an hour left so I was diligent in cleaning the apartment like he left it this morning. By 12:00 pm I donned one of his sweatshirts, complete with my new panties and new shorts. I made a light salad with turkey strips, feta cheese, tomatoes and a light balsamic. Alex's body was perfect just by looking at the contents in his refrigerator. Protein and vegetables were his primary foods, fruits and nuts were secondary. I could not find a loaf of bread in the kitchen or a cracker. He did have some sherbet in the freezer so I crushed up some strawberries in a cup with light cream and let it chill in the refrigerator until he came home.

Everything was set up perfectly by twelve. I called Candy and luckily she was home. She was screaming with delight about all the things I told her. I gave Candy Alex's beeper number in case she needed it and she said, "I leave in four days, when are you coming home?"

I knew that the romance wouldn't last forever so I said, "Probably today."

"Ok, cool," Candy said, "I'll be waiting for you while I pack, don't forget one detail." I said to her in the sweetest sisterly tone, "I love you girl."

Candy was quick to respond and said, "Forget about lovin' me, you better start lovin' that man."

We hung up the phone and within five minutes a key was turning in the door. Alex was so punctual I could hardly contain myself as I met him at the door. When he stepped inside, I had to catch my breath at the sight of him in his uniform. I got protective and said, "What happens when you pull women over?"

"Why do you ask?" Alex said, as he removed his hat and laid it on the coffee table.

"Because, if you pulled me over, I would faint at the very sight of you."

Alex was flattered by my compliment and hugged me tight as he surveyed the room.

"I'm starving, I see you made lunch?"

"Just for you," I said, as I began to pull him to the table. But as

I pulled, he resisted and said, "Come over here, I need to talk to you baby."

I became anxious about what he was going to tell me as he sat down and pulled me between his legs. Alex grabbed my hands as I looked at him. There was longing in his eyes like he wanted me right then and I didn't know what to do. He took his head and buried it in my chest and breathed in all of my energy. He let go of my hands and palmed my butt like a basketball in his manly hands.

"Shanelle, I'm glad you're here, but it's only been four days and I can't get you out of my head. The temptation is too great for me and I want to commit to us being together the right way. I had to ask the Saints to hold onto my will last night with you sleeping in my bed. I wanted to wake you up and make love to you so bad girl."

He cleared his throat and looked up at me like a little boy.

"I couldn't concentrate at work and I need to stay focused on the job."

I stroked the back of his head and neck as he continued to speak to me.

"Did you know that I was sleeping right beside you last night?"

I didn't answer him. Instead, I just stared in his eyes and shook my head no.

"Well, I confess," Alex said. "The need to be near you and to feel you was overwhelming. But I'm not going to jeopardize how you feel."

I looked down at him and kissed his forehead while Alex continued to stroke my butt. I straddled his waist and kissed him long and hard. His face was strained like he needed me in the worst way, even on his lunch hour. I could feel his manhood growing underneath me and it felt overwhelming in strength and size. Alex was so strong he could have easily taken me and fulfilled his need, but I was not ready and we both knew it, no matter how hard we had to resist. With his mighty hands, he hoisted me off his lap and laid me onto the couch. I began to breathe heavily as my breasts ached for his touch. He fulfilled his need only by laying next to me and stroking my legs. He picked up my left leg and stretched it out like an Olympic warm up.

Alex whispered in my ears, "You have the most beautiful legs I have ever seen, next to Flo Jo of course." I laughed at his commentary.

"Ah, Sade forehead, Flo Jo legs, she's turning into a remarkable woman."

Alex laughed uproariously in my ear and then said with a whisper, "Did you like the massage I gave you last night?" I turned and looked at him with surprise, "So that's why I slept so late?" Alex shook his head in agreement and said, "Yes, and that's why you can't stay overnight anymore because the temptation is too great."

I was flattered by his hospitality and said, "Okay, we'll have to plan our weekends better until it's time."

Alex sighed and sat up on the couch. He looked at his pants and said, "I need to take a quick shower just to cool off before I go back to work."

But before he did, we sat down and ate lunch together. I was starving by the time we ate, but I was careful not to wolf my food down. Alex smiled at me every time I held the fork to my mouth. I couldn't understand why, so the next time he did it I paused and said, "What is it?" Alex put his fork down and said, "You need to eat, you're too thin Shanelle."

"Too thin," I replied. "That's an understatement, I already weigh one hundred and thirty five pounds and that's embarrassing." Alex leaned across the table and said, "Trust me, I'm going to get your weight up to one hundred and fifty pounds of pure muscle, just wait and see." My eyes got really wide as I abandoned my plate of food and said, "You're going to have one big fight ahead of you because I don't want to be fat Alex and I mean it." Alex stood up and wiped his mouth in astonishment and said, "Oh, tough girl huh?" I pouted my lips out and hugged him across the table for sympathy.

"I don't want to be any bigger than what I am now, so don't pick on me please." Alex picked me up off the floor and said, "I'm sorry, my little cocoon, I thought you were turning into a butterfly, but I'll wait." Alex put me down on the couch and headed for the door. "I've got to get back, be ready by 4:30 pm and get some more rest, it becomes you." When he left, I pinched my arm to see if I was dreaming and I wasn't. I washed the dishes from lunch and straightened up. I laid down for another hour with the TV on and then slept one hour until 3:00 pm. I packed a few belongings and left a few souvenirs behind for him. Alex came home and took a shower before we left. He noticed sadness in my eyes and cheered me up by singing to me. He loved Magic Man and sang it to me in a deep voice. I laughed all the way to the car as some old people smiled at our hand held happiness. The ride home was all too quick. As soon as we got to the Union Toll, I became quiet and saddened by the fun time I left behind. We I passed the exit for Bloomberg College and asked Alex to take me there to pick up some forms from the Bursar's Office. Alex parked and walked in with me. I was an incoming Freshman and there were plenty of on lookers watching us. He looked at my bill and the names of the classes I was taking. "Interesting, you have the political bug?"

I took the bill from him and only examined the financial damages. "It doesn't matter, I have to get a job so I can pay this bill."

"How much time do you have?" Alex asked.

"I can pay it in three parts and I think I have half of the first payment and that's not including books." Alex sighed and ushered me out the front door and said, "Here, take the keys. I need to use the men's room before I go back to Lakewood. Wait for me in the car."

I took the keys and went back to the car. I looked up and admired the dormitories lined up in front of me. Alex was taking his time, but I didn't care because I didn't want him to leave. As he exited the bursar's, I noticed Alex shoving papers in his back pocket. When he got in the car he said, "Are you smart Shanelle?"

I was puzzled by his question and said, "Yeah when I enjoy the subject." He started the car and said, "Good because it's a shame to waste money on a good education."

We pulled off from the college and I agreed with him. We stopped at the grocery store and Alex bought me some essentials for Candy's house.

He made me carry the bags while he put the cart back. When I got in the car I noticed a piece of paper with the Bloomberg College insignia on the top. I took the paper out as Alex got into the car. He looked at me and said, "No turning back my little cocoon, it's a done deal."

I looked at the paper and opened my mouth with complete surprise. The bill was marked "Paid in Full." I looked at him and said, "Alex, why did you do that?"

He tugged on my ear and said, "Remember Shanelle, if you're not running, then I'm here for you. That only helps us in the future."

I was too shocked to think of an answer. I thanked him as I looked out the window. I wondered if this kind of thing could last forever.

Butterfly

By fall of 1984, I was nestled in the comfort of Alex and his loving ways. I embraced my classes without rebellion or scorn. Little communication came from home because my brother was still there. Mom and Dad were absorbed in silence and sent subliminal messages in cards and phone messages. They were happy I was in school and pursuing my future goals, but they were also hoping that we could really get together and be a family. By that time, I had experienced so much of Alex's uncomplicated routine world, it was easy to ignore my emptiness. I made the honor roll and filled out an application to St. James University for my Sophomore year. Alex paid my bills and dorm fees. The happiness I felt inside increased my weight to one hundred and fifty pounds without missing a beat. I had more curves and muscle mass and Alex bragged that he didn't have to force feed me to gain weight. Since I was sleeping at his apartment again, he picked me up every Saturday and brought me home after the Sunday beach traffic died down. In between visits to his family, the Fosters whispered behind our backs about how much we were in love and wondered when we would get married.

By March, I received an acceptance letter from St. James University. I was elated because they had a great English Department and I wanted desperately to become a writer. Alex begged me to write poetry and bought a camera to take pictures of me while I scripted pen to paper. Each time we went to his apartment, simple treasures of our love were everywhere. Alex had so many photographs of me that a psychologist would have termed it a "Narcissist's delight and a stalker's dream gallery." Candy was nestled in Pittsburg having the time of her life and begging for money each week. I usually called her from Alex's house every Saturday, but Miss Party Girl was having so much fun, I abandoned the phone calls and we started writing letters to each other. Candy knew the momentum was building between us. She told me that the "first time" would hurt. She also said that when the pain subsided, making love to Alex would feel like pure pleasure.

Alex and I were in the "I love you" stages. He wanted me to transfer to Ocean County and take classes in the Fall but I ignored his request. There were signs of an unofficial engagement everywhere we went including the gleamy smiles everyone gave us.

By June of 1985, our love blossomed into a full courtship and the intensity of us making love grew deeper and stronger. I wanted him inside of me in the worst way. The calendar cycled me into full bloom by the July 4th weekend. We planned a quiet and early day at the beach with the new bikes we purchased at Sears. They were matching twelve speeds made out of a lightweight aluminum frame. We worked out together every Saturday and Sunday morning. The consistency in our routine pumped my legs up to marathon status and Alex loved to admire them with his strong hands. In his heart he said that I was a fearless woman warrior with the backbone to prove it and he would be proud to call me his wife. There were many nights that I wanted to give myself to him, but he told me no because he wanted his cocoon to begin to blossom and he would not give in. The weekend before the July 4th weekend was intense for the both of us. I took a shower with Alex and I knew that I was in trouble by his size and wondered if I could truly make him happy. He washed my hair and kissed me long and hard and told me that it was going to hurt, but he loved me and wouldn't do anything to make me feel unloved by his touch. I cried in his arms at the thought of going through the experience with him while he caressed me. He carried me to the bed and rubbed me down with my favorite Jasmine oil. Alex spread my legs as he whispered in my ear and said, "This is just the beginning of our lives and I want you to feel love from me in a pleasurable way before we make love." His touch from below sent me into pure ecstasy and engorgement. I felt light headed and crazy as he made love to Kitty. A sensation stirred from my head to my toes until a release came from my organs that trembled and pulsated me into an abyss of coital pleasure. I called his name as he slowed down for me to take in the entire sensation. I was so overwhelmed with pleasure I began to shake all over as Alex held me tight. My head felt empty and my nipples were erect. My mouth was so dry Alex had to bring me some water. Afterwards, I turned on my side in a fetal position as Alex rested behind me. He was so erect that he had to put his loins between my thighs to relieve himself as he called my name. I knew the pleasure he shared with me that night heightened my need to be one with him as he called my name in intense pleasure. We took a shower together and he knew that I needed to relax by myself so he turned the shower into a bath and added some bath beads. He washed my back and said, "I think

I'm going to call you butterfly."

I leaned my head back on the tub and said, "Yes, you're right."

July 4th came and the stage was set for my liberation. I was in full bloom and I was happy with my body for once in my life. I bought a new bathing suit and beach cover up so Alex could take some more photographs of me. We parked our bikes and I went into the McDonalds to change. When I came out Alex's eyes popped open at the site of my black and white bikini and fishnet cover up. It was the first time I felt confident enough to wear a bikini and by the look on his face, he was glad I was wearing it for him. When I looked up at him he said, "Shanelle, don't think you're going to wear that again, but let me get some shots of you just in case I forget what you looked like."

An early morning party was taking place across the street. Drunken hecklers poised on top of their rooftop were just as excited as Alex was to see me strike a pose. One of them started clapping and shouted, "You go brown sugar!" I wasn't phased and neither was Alex. I put my glasses on and slid down the wall for the last shot and said, "I'm ready."

Alex perched down and said, "For me butterfly?" I raised my hand in the air and perched the other over my head and said, "Yes, for you Alex." The shutter released and the picture was taken like a memorialized treasure on the Fourth of July. I walked up to him and said, "Well, you can't say I didn't do what you said."

He looked puzzled as I said, "Take the Parkway South to exit 98 and bring those big pretty legs with you."

Alex laughed as we exchanged high fives. The drunken guys on the roof across the street, bellowed out in a drunken slur, "You go brother!"

We shook our heads and headed for the beach.

We laid on our beach towels as Alex whispered sweet nothings in my ear. The tide was rough that morning but we were ready for the thrill. Alex swam into the deep water and I followed behind. He stood neck deep in the water as I swam to him and wrapped my legs around him. He looked me in the eyes, and asked, "Are you sure Shanelle?"

Suddenly, a six foot wave came out of nowhere and took us under. Alex came up first and pulled me up as we laughed and swam closer to shore. The lifeguard began calling people in and then to the center. I wrapped myself around his waist as he knelt down in the water and kissed me. The water glistened off his skin and I remembered how handsome he looked to me that day.

Alex explored me underwater and joked, "That's not a jelly fish down there is it?"

I laughed and said, "No, that's good old Shanelle gel, you can't even get this stuff at the store."

Alex looked confident and said, "Is it all mine?"

I nodded yes as another wave hit us but I knew that he saw my answer. I found him again and asked, "Are you sure Alex Foster?"

Alex replied and said, "Just as sure as you're going to be Mrs. Alex Foster."

I felt a love pain that knotted in my stomach as tears came down my face and said, "I love you Alex. I love your stability, honesty, spirituality and that I am giving myself to you with love, and commitment." I couldn't finish because another wave knocked us down. Alex picked me up and said, "You should write that down, you really learned something at that expensive college."

I looked at him and replied, "From you, I learned that love is the air that fills my lungs and gives me life and I want you to release life into me."

Alex wiped the salty water away from my eyes and stared at me with honest intentions and said, "Let's go home Shanelle and lock ourselves away."

I stood motionless as I looked at my erect nipples and said, "Alex wait."

He looked surprised and said, "What is it?" I pointed at a article of clothing in the water.

"No wonder you felt Shanelle gel, my top is floating over there."

He started to laugh as I stooped down in the water. Belmar was not a nudist beach as far as I knew, but I wasn't going to give any one a peep show except for my dream guy Alex. I knelt down in the water as Alex swam back to me. I turned around and he put the bikini top back on my naked frame. He whispered sweet nothings in my ear and I felt like we were the eighth wonder of the world. The mighty warrior stood in front of me while I climbed on his back and he proudly carried his fair maiden from the excited onlookers. I buried my head while a few of Alex's abandoned acquaintances whistled and clapped. Alex walked up the embankment and carried me to the boardwalk. I was covered with sandy residue from the pounding ocean. I watched my warrior go back and retrieve our belongings. He was everything I wanted and needed in my life. Alex walked up the stairs and I put on my white beach coverup and smiled. He put my hood on and said, "Such an appropriate color for you today my butterfly. You look beautiful."

A tear ran down my face in pure excitement as he knelt down to put my sandals on my feet. As we walked back to his Mazda, the holiday revelers filled up Belmar Beach to maximum capacity. A young couple beeped and waved as Alex signaled them to come to our parking space. They were blasting The Police from their car stereo and looked as blissfully happy. Alex gave the guy his beach pass and ticket and they shook hands as I put my bag in the trunk. Alex escorted me to the passenger side and opened the door for me. I began to brush the sandy residue from my body but Officer Foster said, "Freeze young lady, that won't be necessary."

I looked at him with bedroom eyes and wondered if he knew about my fantasy.

"Am I under arrest officer?"

Alex put his lips to mine and sealed it with the kiss. He looked at me and said, "I'm taking you into custody for at least three days and your cooperation will be expected."

I rubbed my thumb across his mouth and said, "Three days?" Alex held my hand as I got into the car and closed the door. He got in on his side and said, "You've been a very good girl for me, so yes, three days." I didn't utter a word. I repositioned my seat and laid back at a forty degree angle. Alex put on Sade and I looked up into the sky. Despite the beautiful morning, gray storm clouds were floating up above. I put on my glasses and closed my eyes as Alex drove away. The excitement of his touch began to arouse my senses as he shifted the gears and made contact with my inner thighs. He drove to the grocery store while I relaxed in the car. As he was standing at the register, I stared at him with small pangs of pleasure. I crossed my legs and stared out the window. The sun was going away as the dark cloud rested above me. I held my hand out to stretch and noticed my garnet ring, so delicate in appearance. The prisms were deep and hard to gage as I twisted my hand from side to side. The surface was hard and the redness was deep and thick as the multiple prisms hid secrets like a buried treasure. I caressed my ring and ran my thumb across the beautiful stone. I looked at Alex through the window as he paid the cashier. I looked back at the ring with a tear of joy in my eye and suddenly an old friend came to visit. In a soft sultry voice she said,

"Hello Shanelle."

I closed my eyes and said in my mind, "Greetings Nemesis."

She replied, "Greetings indeed. I've been quiet for a few months butterfly, but I come to you with love and concern as you appear to be like the lioness in full estrus."

I ran my fingers across my chest and took a deep breath. Alex exited the store and I was in awe of his entire presence as he winked at me. The song advanced to “Your Love is King” and Nemesis replied,

"Check well young lioness that you are protected from his seeds of life, perhaps a Trojan or two will do the trick."

I closed my eyes and said, "I know, we are both responsible."

"I don't doubt your intentions, young love child, but the love you feel will surely cloud your judgments as he enters your soul with pain and pleasure."

Alex got in the car and stared at me. "Is everything ok baby?"

I shook my head as he handed me a bouquet of flowers that went unnoticed in my exchange with Nemesis. "These are beautiful Alex, thank you."

The close proximity to the scent of the flowers and my thoughts of making love to Alex overwhelmed me and I started to cry. He immediately grabbed me despite the awkwardness of his bucket seats.

"Shhhh, Shanelle, don't cry, it's going to be okay. Why are you crying?"

I buried my face into his neck and continued to cry.

"I just love you so much and I need to know that everything is going to be okay. I mean, I know that it is but…"

Alex quieted me down as he stroked my back.

"Just say the word Shanelle and we'll wait, I told you before, I love you and I wouldn't do anything that you're not ready to handle butterfly."

The tight squeeze around Alex's neck revealed the red garnet, so beautiful and delicate. I let go of Alex and looked him in the eyes. He was calm, mature and steady as he wiped my tears with his thumb. I grabbed his hand as he continued to stroke my face. I searched his eyes into his soul and trust was there completely. I focused and looked at him with serious intentions as I placed his thumb in my mouth and suckled it ever so gently. His face was filled with pain and I knew that I wanted him to make love to me. I let go of him and nestled back into the seat and said, "Let's go, it looks like a soft and wonderful thunderstorm is headed this way."

Without a word Alex started the car as Sade escorted us home. Alex brought the groceries inside while I put the flowers in a vase. His apartment had slowly become mixed with hints of estrogen that complimented the kitchen, living room and bedroom. I brought the flowers into the bedroom and looked around. I went to the closet and took out a cream laced cloth and put it on the nightstand. The flowers complimented the scenery. Shades of darkness rolled into the window as Alex came in to close the windows. He came from behind me and said, "I love the rain."

I turned around and said, "I love you."

Alex kissed my neck and said, "Well maybe after I make love to you, you'll love the rain as much as I do."

I went back into the living room and by the looks of things Alex took care of business. Condoms were sitting on the countertop and I sighed with relief. I began to close the living room blinds as darkness fell upon the room. Alex came into the living room and took the phone off the hook. I smiled like an innocent college freshman and looked at the clock. It was 1:00 pm and serenity rested in the room. Alex turned the air conditioner down and I put the teakettle on for tea. I asked him if he wanted some and he politely said no as he walked up behind me and kissed my neck. I turned around to face him and as soon as I did Alex swept me off my feet. I was so dazed and confused by his touch that spasms shot through my body. Alex carried me into the bathroom as I stared into his eyes. There was an intense sensual pain in my stomach as Alex lifted my beach coverup over my head. I closed my eyes and bit my lips from his touch as he peeled my bikini off. Seaweed and sand salt stuck to my behind as Alex applied cold water to his hands and applied pressure with small circles. Then he picked me up and sat me on top of the bathroom countertop. He removed my sandals and wiped the debris from off my feet. He washed his hands as a burst of thunder and lightening rang outside. Alex stared at me as I looked in his eyes. He kissed my cheeks, nose, ears and neck. I held his head and received his warm and inviting touch. He grabbed my left hand and stared at the ring. My hands were slightly swollen as he stroked the ruby red gem. He poured some liquid soap in his hands and applied it to his fingertips. He rubbed it around the perimeter of the gold band and on top of my finger. Then he took his other hand and pressed his thumb into the garnet. His pointer finger supported the back of my finger as he slid the ring off and put it on the glass cabinet shelf. Tears trickled down my face as he kissed each one away and said, "You're safe with me Shanelle, I'm yours' for life. I can't believe that you are finally my precious gem."

He comforted me as he stroked and kissed my face tenderly.

"I promise to treat you like a precious and delicate butterfly, but if you want me to stop, just tell me and I will."

My breathing began to calm as I placed my arms around him in complete trust. We talked about this day for so long and I knew that Alex was going to respect each and every moment. Alex lifted me off the countertop with one hand. He turned on the shower as cold water whimsically flowed from the faucet head. Darkness fell upon the room like the sky on a dreamy night. He lifted me into the shower as goose bumps overwhelmed my senses. My nipples froze from the cold water as Alex washed away the sandy residue. I was alert and in full focus. Alex turned the hot water on as the element turned to a deluge of warm pulsating pellets. He knelt down as I held onto the glass door. Alex began to kiss my ankles as he ran his hands up my inner thigh. I called his name, but he lulled me into silence with a firm kiss to my inner thigh. The excitement from his exploratory kiss weakened my knees to rest in his shoulders. He pressed his hand into my stomach and claimed my physiology. Alex turned the water into a bath and stepped out of the tub. He increased the temperature by adding hot water to the mildly warm pool of water floating to the surface of my calves and thighs. He went to the cabinet and took out my favorite bath beads fragranced in orange citrus. I grabbed the Cream of Nature Shampoo and caressed it into my damp hair. Alex went in the room and came back with my favorite candle and a cup of peppermint tea. He placed the candle in the corner of the tub as I sipped the hot substance. I placed the tea on the floor because I was too overwhelmed by his touch to concentrate on fluids. I held my head back as he rinsed the shampoo from my hair. Curls and waves sprang up everywhere as he massaged my scalp. The soapy water turned to creamy milk as Alex rinsed my hair out. He went into the room and came back with a silk satchel. He opened it up and laid rose petals on my nipples and waited for each rise in my stomach to lay more on my chest. He put the bag down as I continued to receive the pleasure of his touch. His caress was unforgiving as he slid his hands onto my big glorious thighs he so loved. I quietly whispered, "I love you Alex, I love you."

Alex said nothing as he looked into my eyes. He pushed the stopper down and turned on the water and washed my entire frame with the creamy soap. He looked at me and said, "So beautiful, so pure, my butterfly." I tried to speak, but he quieted me with his fingers. Alex took a dry cloth and wiped the steamy residue from my face and temples. He pulled the tiny curls that sprang from the base and temple of my hair behind my ears. Alex got up and opened our new white Ralph Lauren towels. They were thick and plush as I stood up to receive him. He patted my face again and then placed the towel behind me as I appeared exposed in the front. Alex took one last look at my frame and said, "Wrap up butterfly."

Alex helped me step on the dry plush carpet and picked me up like a delicate swan. He carried me to the bed and placed me directly in the middle of the king size mattress. The smooth cotton sheets felt warm as I searched for the sound of the quiet rain outside. Alex went into the kitchen and came back with a basket of strawberries. The first bite was sweet as Alex used his thumb to force the juices back into my mouth. He crushed a strawberry in his manly hands and carried it to Kitty's den as she purred and cooed with sensual delight. I closed my eyes as Alex traveled there with untold pleasure as my body rhythmically guided his tongue. Tears flowed uncontrollably as he enticed Kitty into an erotic spasm. I dug my nails into his flesh out of pleasure and not pain. Alex reached his hand out to me as we locked hands in a committed embrace. Intensity grew in my nipples as I began to release my self from his touch. He rested his head on my stomach and took a deep breath. I cried his name and spoke to him in unknown languages. He squeezed my hand back to answer me as I relaxed into a quiet breathing rhythm. He came back to me and buried his face in my neck as I said things I didn't mean like, "I hate you, don't do this, why did you do that to me?"

Alex grabbed my hand and said, "I'm here baby, I'm not going anywhere."

Alex laid his head on my stomach and stroked my swollen womb. He kissed the places that tiny seeds would one day grow and mature into being. He kissed my belly button and stroked my thighs as I cried into my hands. He received me again into his mouth and I was dazed and confused by his touch. I could feel Alex's manhood against me and the strength of him made me breathe rhythmically. I called his name and said, "I want you, take me Alex, I want to feel you inside of me."

Alex got up and put a strawberry in his mouth. He shifted the strawberry into the corner and looked at me with a devilish grin as he bit into the sweet fruit. Walking strong and proud, Alex went into the bathroom and started singing Magic Man to lighten the mood as I giggled with delight. I could here him gargling over the faucet as the rain began to fall harder outside. He turned on the shower and began to sing. He turned a Chilite classic into a song for me exclaiming, "Shanelle is so delicious." The hard pellets outside increased with intensity as a drum beat ceremony romanced us. Alex entered the room with a white towel wrapped around his waist. He took a condom off the nightstand and slid next to me. He pulled me on top of him as I straddled his waist, unsure of what he wanted me to do first. I looked at him and his face appeared so calm and reassuring like the world around us was standing still. I removed his towel as he followed my eyes and hands. His face was strained as he reached out and stroked my neck. I watched Alex protect us from seeds of life that we were not ready for in our world. Alex sat up and gently laid my shoulders back on the bed as I began to breathe heavily. He placed his hand on my stomach to calm me and said, "Breathe through your nose Shanelle and relax baby."

I trusted him as I placed my hands at my side. Alex placed his body on top of mine and whispered love and affection through his calm breath. He whispered a brief preamble before he took me.

"Breathe Shanelle, just breathe. Hold onto me for support. It's going to hurt baby so hold onto me and bite me if you don't want to cry."

He began to enter me and said, "If you want me to stop I will. It's going to take time to feel pleasure over the pain. But I love you and the pain you feel is a natural part of your existence."

Alex took my arms and relaxed my grip around his neck so he could position himself. I looked in his eyes and was comforted by his calm as the intensity started to build in a sharp piercing pain. As Alex slowly entered me it felt like my flesh was being torn in agony as I dug my nails into him from the pronounced pain. I began to cry as he lulled my pain through the main prism. Each prism became more and more penetrable and was met with unimaginable pain. Alex took his time as I closed my eyes and sunk into depths of small pleasure which came in quick spurts and then pain pierced it back down as he went deep inside me. I began to bite his flesh as Alex whispered, "Hold me Shanelle, hurt me if you have to."

I cried his name as he rhythmically moved in and out of my swollen cavity. As tears continued to flow, Alex kissed each one away and asked me if I wanted him to stop. I pulled him in closer to negate his doubt. He looked in my eyes with a strained face as he called my name. "Shanelle, we are finally one baby, I love you, I love you girl."

Alex called my name over and over again as he caressed one of my treasured legs. He looked at me and said, "Don't ever leave me Shanelle, I'll die if you leave me girl."

I cried for his sensitivity and compassion. He began to enjoy being inside of me as he made love to every inch of my soul. I cried softly as small bits of pleasure began to rise up with the comfort in his voice and the oneness of our flesh. We embraced under the musical orchestra of the falling rain. I began to stroke his back and call his name as Alex started to release his precious seeds. He called my name as his body collapsed and crushed my frame. He buried his head in my neck and said, "My sweet butterfly."

He kissed my neck and stomach as he held my hand. Remnants of our love soiled the fabric that laid beneath us. Alex lifted me up and carried me to the tub. He had prepared a cool cucumber bath that was waiting for me as he placed me in the tub. I closed my eyes as he rinsed me down with soft circular motions. The cool water and soaking cucumbers enticed me into a delicate rest as I looked at the fullness of my body. Alex sat beside me and held my hand in the quiet darkness. I stared back at him and stroked his face with trust and tenderness. Alex took the tea I left behind and prepared a fresh cup. While I drank the tea, he changed the linens and turned off the air conditioner. He turned on a light jazz radio station and sat with me while I drank my tea. After a twenty minute soak, I felt at ease to stand up and dry off. I looked in the mirror and smiled at myself while Alex held me from behind. Our faces merged together like a beautiful picture book of chocolate love. We climbed back in bed as Alex massaged my legs with baby oil. Afterwards, he massaged my scalp with his large hands. My eyes became restless as he stroked my fingers. He pulled my body into his so I could rest in between his legs. He also rubbed the empty place my garnet laid for so many years and whispered in my ear.

"Where once a garnet wrapped to protect, a pear shaped diamond laid to rest."

I smiled at the romantic play on words, but I was too tired to find meaning in his verbiage. Alex rocked me into a quiet respite as I began to fall asleep in his arms. He stroked his fingertips across my back and pushed the covers back to admire my frame. I lapsed into an infantile sleep as Alex began to stir up a need to be with him again. This time he lulled his tongue into me for fifteen glorious minutes until I experienced a second rush of ecstasy. I turned to the side crying and overwhelmed by the power of the experienced as he wrapped me up in his sheets. I went back to sleep as Alex went into the bathroom for another shower. I slept for three hours under the patter of falling rain. I felt Alex slide next to me clothed with cotton underwear. I did not wake up because I sensed he was fulfilled for now. He pulled me into his frame and stroked my temples forcing me into deeper sleep. After a four hour rest, I woke up to the sounds of fireworks. The loud thunderous noise pierced red and blue light images through the blinds. Alex snuggled in closer to me as I pulled his arms in tighter to hold me. I stroked his beautiful cinnamon skin and smiled with the embrace of our love. I turned around to face him and nestled my head under his neck. I whispered to him, "Are you awake Alex?" Alex shook his head and said, "No, I'm in love Mrs. Foster." I giggled at his confidence and said, "Mrs. Foster, or soon to be Mrs. Foster?" Alex laughed with a deep and groggy voice and said, "You're right, you're right, I stand corrected, soon to be Mrs. Foster."

I pushed myself back in order to comfortably wrap my arms around him as we nestled under the sheets. I called his name in a soft whisper as I reached my arms out to hold him. Just then, a sparkle flashed as I wrapped my hands around his neck. I held my head up and to my surprise a pear shaped diamond decorated my ring finger. Then I understood the meaning of his riddled words. I gasped as Alex held my hand up and said, "Say yes, Shanelle." Tears of joy streamed down my face as I proclaimed, "Yes, Alex."

We hugged for what seemed to be an eternity as the fireworks resounded with a grand finale. Alex kissed me all over as our twelve month courtship brought the two of us into one being. He became enticed by my touch and I commanded his love into me again. The pain was beginning to subside as he called my name and held me tight. The time spent making love was without a shield of protection as tiny seeds of life were released into me. We ended our evening with a hot soaking bath and quiet conversation. Alex rested against me as I rubbed his chest with warm creamy soap. The candle burning in the corner symbolized eternity as Alex committed his love and devotion to me. As our water laced ceremony continued, I in turn made a promise of long lasting commitment. The evening was complimented with buttery pancakes in bed. I ate heartily as Alex spread syrup across my lips and licked his fingers. I looked at him with happiness as my life intertwined with his. I cleaned up the breakfast dishes while Alex called his mother and announced that we had something special to tell her at tomorrow's family gathering. I went back to bed as I massaged my swollen stomach with my right hand and held my pear shaped diamond up in the air. I wrapped my arms around myself with clear vision and then closed my eyes into a peaceful and quiet rest. Alex took a call from the station and rested on the side of the bed. He kissed my forehead and said he would be back in one hour. I shook my head with fatigue. Whatever he said was barely audible as I lay wrapped under our covers.

I drifted off to sleep and *walked through a quiet meadow. There were two black puppies that looked like Kiko. They licked my face like little children enjoying delicious ice cream on a sunny day. I put them down and took a deep breath as they scampered up a grassy hill. The grass felt warm beneath my toes as I sat down and laid back into the green scenery.* Warm delicious smells were all around me as I felt someone touch my face. I opened my eyes temporarily. Alex was back and filled the room with white gardenias and a strawberry fruit basket. I smiled at the sight of them and looked up at Alex with loving eyes. He kissed my cheeks and said, "I love you, welcome home butterfly."

Beauty so serene has a fatal flaw. Tune in...

Acknowledgments

Moody's Soap Box

My friends have become so busy these days in our "fast lane" lives. The question most frequently asked of me when we do have time to chat is, "When did you decide to write a book?" Hopefully, I won't have to repeat the answer too many times, but here is the answer:

At the age of four, my mother enrolled me in a private preschool in Manhattan. Every morning, she would gently rub my shoulders and tell me it was time to wake up. The notion of waking up before the sun seemed silly to me, but I was a compliant Capricorn child. I boarded a yellow school bus with the rest of my sleepy preschool mates as we headed to Manhattan. The boy seated behind me constantly pulled my hair and said awful things to me like, "You're a stupid head, I hate you." In my adult life, I figured out that he was expressing his innocent affection for me, but at the time, it felt cruel and calculating.

When the bus arrived at my school, two preschool teachers received us at the door. I was the unlucky one who had the mean teacher with piercing eyes. She called us her "flock," as she pushed our shoulders into perfect linear formation. Because I was taller than the rest of my preschool mates, I was instructed to stand in the back of the line. She never let me stand in the front, or be the line leader. I remembered feeling angry and wishing that I was in the "nice teacher's" class.

The most prominent memory of my preschool experience was my teacher's constant recital of the Lord's Prayer. She repeated the prayer so many times that the words began to form stories in my head. I remembered thinking, "There's a bad sheep herder in the valley. He hides in the shadows with a rod. I don't ever want to go to the valley, someone died in there." In fact, her constant reference to the "Shepard," formed the first belief of what I wanted to be when I grew up. I told everyone until the age of nine that I wanted to be a veterinarian. In my mind, there were lots of sick animals in the world.

I never told my mother. In fact, all I wanted to do was to be a good student and do what I was told. I never stepped out of bounds because it seemed to be the right thing to do at the time. There's an old saying that goes, "Children should be seen and not heard." Well, the things I have heard over the course of my childhood have certainly affected the person that I have become. Good, bad or indifferent, children need to be heard. They need a voice, a mentor, a hug, a role model and consistent nurturing.

Lastly, the Lord's Prayer is an awesome prayer. The sweetest rendition was introduced to me after I purchased the Whitney Houston soundtrack from the Preacher's Wife. Dare I say that the eloquent voice of Cissy Houston, along with the Hezekiah Walker Choir filled my eyes with glorified tears. Now, the valley looks greener and the Shepard is awesome. Thank you, Moody Holiday.

To Mario, So much of who of I am is because of you. I love you.

Mom, So stoic and regal, know that I will always love you.

Charles and Vollie, Grandparents are special indeed.

Kyle and family, Hold it together and keep moving forward.

Candy, What can I say, after twenty-four years of friendship we're still laughing like the good old days. Watch the closing doors, another one will open.

Mo, The fierce competitor and sensitive soul sister, what a great mommy you have become. Remember to box out and work on your three pointer. See you on the court.

Bonnie, The long walk home was a blast, especially the chocolate chip mint ice cream. Could it get any better than that?

Cindy, Stop borrowing my clothes and get my room ready. Here's another laugh, How's the rice? Cakes, cookies and pies, oh my!

Angie, Thanks for the laughs and putting up with moody me in the dorm room. Also, thanks for going home every weekend.

Brie, Lady Soul who shoots straight from the hip, you tell it like it is Brooklyn style. I love you.

Ladies in the "L" Wing: Magali, T.R. A.S. aka "Sexy Mama" Great detective work, love ya!

1993 & 2003 TPZ crew including P.W., Lady Di, J.H. Big Lou, A.R, H.F., don't forget my chocolate at 3:00 pm.

Legal Eagle Sarno, Thanks for the phone call, you are a sweetheart.

Mercie me, What would I do without you? Big sister indeed.

Anita, You are a phenomenal woman and I love you for being you.

Leonard and Mary, Thanks for everything. Sorry about the

window.

JC, Thank you for your endless attention, there is safety in flight.

Rita, More macaroni and cheese please, do your thang girl!

D&L, Thanks for the quiet solace in Rhode Island, see you soon. We love you.

D. McMorrin, What can I say, I didn't want to go, but you made the law sound so exciting. Thanks for lending your ear counselor.

Daba, Here comes the hot pepper! Thanks for the read and the good laughs. Another down to earth sister in my corner.

Blanche and Naomi, Thanks for being a big sister to me.

To all my Godchildren: B.B., D.F., L.B. aka Fragglerock, Ms. M in Tampa, you are my stars. Stay committed to the things that make you whole.

Sisters Computer Systems: Thank you for your professionalism.

The Pacesetters, Always in my heart, see you at the next dinner.

Peace and Blessings to all, Love Moody.